DISCOVER

Mysteries of the past and present

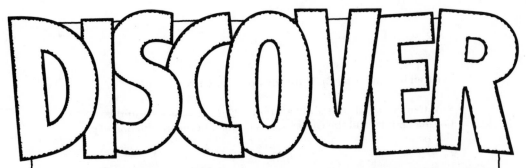

DISCOVER
Mysteries of the past and present

ROM
A ROYAL ONTARIO MUSEUM BOOK

BY KATHERINE GRIER
Illustrations by Pat Cupples

KIDS CAN PRESS LTD.
TORONTO

Written by Katherine Grier for the Royal Ontario Museum.

Kids Can Press Ltd. gratefully acknowledges the assistance of the Canada Council and the Ontario Arts Council in the production of this book.

CANADIAN CATALOGUING IN PUBLICATION DATA

Main entry under title:

Discover: mysteries of the past and present

Includes index.
ISBN 0-921103-55-7 (bound) ISBN 0-921103-86-7 (pbk.)

1. Museums - Juvenile literature. 2. Museum techniques - Juvenile literature. 3. Civilization - Juvenile literature. 4. Creative activities and seat work - Juvenile literature. I. Royal Ontario Museum. II. Cupples, Patricia.

AM7.D58 1989   j069.5   C89 = 093180-1

Edited by Valerie Wyatt
Book design by Nancy Ruth Jackson
Typeset by Compeer Typographic Services Limited
Printed and bound in Canada by John Deyell Company

89 0 9 8 7 6 5 4 3 2 1

Contents

For Megan Fehlberg
who delights in small things,
natural and otherwise

Acknowledgements

Many people at the Royal Ontario Museum spoke with me about their work, briefly or at length and repeatedly. Some went over my drafts and caught errors that crept in as I tried to write simply about complex things. My thanks to all of them: Maria Arts, Brian Beattie, Naomi Beirnes, Pat Bolland, Rosemary Burd, Sandy Bushell, Jeanne Cannizzo, Angela Cheng, Des Collins, Tim Dickinson, Ewa Dziadowiec, Alison Easson, Jim Eckenwalder (at the University of Toronto), Julia Fenn, Georgette Frampton, Ruth Freeman, Helmuth Fuchs, Jessica Hallett, Elizabeth Hayes, John Hayes, Mary Hayes, Robert Henrickson, Sona Henrickson, Adrienne Hood, Dana Leigh Hopson, Jack Howard, Brian Iwama, Art Jamieson, Marilyn Jenkins, Ed Keall, Corey Keeble, Shyh-charng Lo, Mima Kapches, Ken Lister, Julia Matthews, Jock McAndrews, Jim McDonald, Brian Mussel-white, Trudy Nicks, Alexandra Palmer, Monica Paul, David Pendergast, Bill Pratt, Patty Proctor, So Ying Quan, Barbara Soren, Susan Stock, Ka Bo Tsang, Vince Vertolli, Hugh Wylie, Brian Young. My special thanks to: Arni Brownstone, Janet Cowan, Peta Daniels, Julie Frost, Claire Loughheed, Deb Metsger, Margaret Pickles, Elaine Rousseau, Kevin Seymour, Roberta Shaw, Janet Waddington and Susan Woodward. Thanks to my colleague Dan Yashinsky. And thanks to my neighbours, Young S. Kim, Dongjo Kim and Richard Sopala, who told me how they played as children in Korea and Poland.

Hugh Porter, head of the ROM Publications Department, helped me find my way through the maze behind the scenes at the Museum. ROM editor Mary Terziano made many helpful suggestions.

My friend and editor, Valerie Wyatt, somehow managed to be understanding and ruthless at the same time. Larry MacDonald helped me come to grips with computers. Other friends and members of my family listened critically, especially: Arlene Anisman, Amy Bodman, Maggie Fehlberg, Martha Grier, Muriel and William Grier, Marion Jacklin, Rita Johnson, Celia Lottridge, Helen Porter and Frieda and Bill Wishinsky. I appreciated their comments and encouragement deeply.

What's a museum?

What's a museum? Try to answer that question and you can be sure of one thing. There's no simple answer. That's because there's much more to a museum than meets the eye. A whole lot is going on behind the scenes. Dip into this book and see for yourself.

- Try out some of the observing and collecting tricks museum scientists use "in the field."
- Tease yourself with some museum puzzles and problems.
- Find out a little more about your ancestors and the creatures that lived before them on the earth.
- Sample some of the tasks and crafts and customs that were part of daily life long ago.

Expand your mind. Who knows—your museum may never seem quite the same again.

Before you start

You'll be able to do most of the activities in this book in a few minutes or hours. A few take much longer to finish. When you see what they are, you'll understand why. You'll be copying processes that happen in nature. In fact, sometimes you'll really speed them up.

GOBBLEDEGOOK?

Some words that tell what people do in museums can look like gobbledegook. Don't give up! Turn to the glossary on page 92 to find out what they mean.

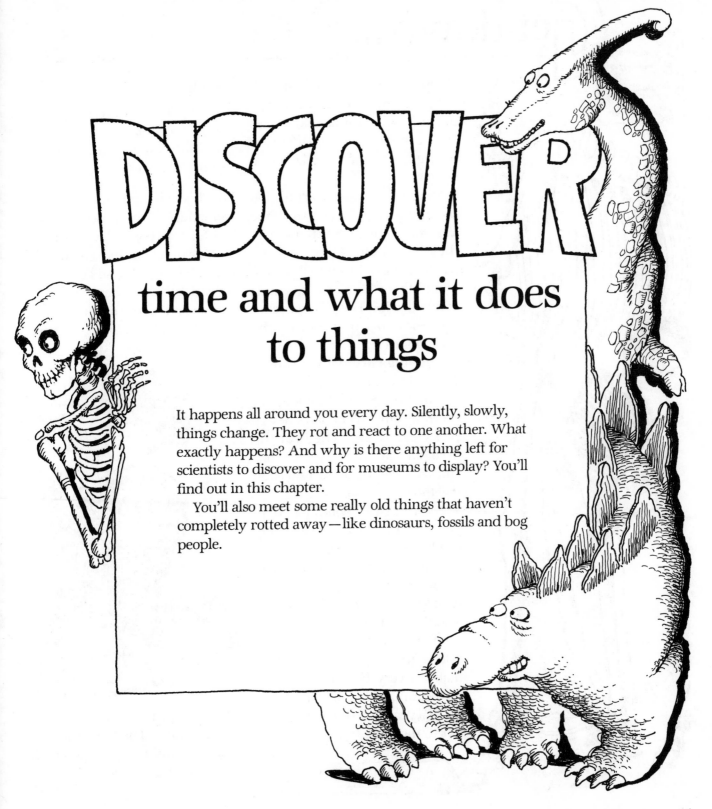

DISCOVER

time and what it does to things

It happens all around you every day. Silently, slowly, things change. They rot and react to one another. What exactly happens? And why is there anything left for scientists to discover and for museums to display? You'll find out in this chapter.

You'll also meet some really old things that haven't completely rotted away—like dinosaurs, fossils and bog people.

Get down...

If you've ever wandered through a museum, you've probably noticed some animal skeletons. Have you ever wondered how the museum got those skeletons so clean?

Museum scientists start the job by cutting most of the flesh off the skeletons. But to finish the job, they need help. They take the partly cleaned skeletons to a "bug room" that's home to thousands of tiny beetles. The young beetles need meat to grow. They eat the skeletons clean.

The bugs are dainty eaters. They can clean even a bat wing or a hummingbird skull without breaking any tiny bones. They're picky eaters too. They eat the flesh but leave the tough tendons and cartilage that hold a skeleton together.

You can clean bones too, only you won't be using meat-eating beetles. You'll be using bacteria, the tiniest living natural cleaners of all. They are much too small for us to see but they're all around us — in the air, the earth, the water, even on and inside us. The only catch is that even a small skeleton makes a very big meal for such tiny cleaners. It will take them about a year to do their work. It's worth the wait.

You'll need:

o *a jar with a wide top and a screw-on lid*
o *a small nail and a hammer*
o *a trowel or shovel*

1. Choose a specimen. Try something from the kitchen with lots of bones, like a small fish or part of a chicken. Make sure the bones are still connected to each other. It's better not to use a dead mouse or bird that you find outside. Bacteria won't eat tough fur and skin.

2. Cut or pick most of the meat off the bones. The more the bacteria have to eat, the longer it will take them to clean the bones.

...to the bare bones

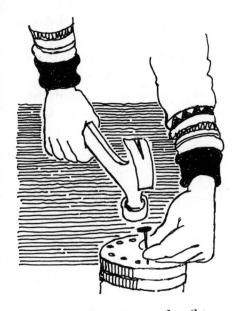

3. Use the hammer and nail to knock about 20 little holes (about this big ●) in the lid of your jar. Put several holes quite close together along one edge of the lid as shown. (Don't forget the holes. They allow the liquid caused by decay to escape. Some museum collectors once buried a bear carcass inside several big green garbage bags. They forgot the holes. They got bear soup, not a clean skeleton.)

4. Put your specimen in the jar and screw the lid on tightly. Wash your hands with soap.

5. Dig a hole in the ground about as deep as your forearm. Put your jar in this hole. Lay it on its side and turn it till the part of the lid with the most holes is lowest. Fill in the hole. Make sure you know where it is.

6. Wait for about a year. Dig up the jar. You should find a skeleton that's almost clean. Rinse it gently in water to finish the job. The skeleton is delicate. Store it in a box to keep it safe. Wash your hands with soap after handling your bacteria bottle.

How does a bacteria bottle work? The small holes in the lid let bacteria in—but not worms or bugs that might break the skeleton. The holes also let liquid caused by decay out. Like the beetles in the bug room, the bacteria are dainty, picky eaters. They eat the tender flesh before nibbling on the tougher parts that hold the skeleton together.

ROOF ROT

In the old days, scientists at the Royal Ontario Museum took animal carcasses up to the museum roof. There they were cleaned by the bacteria in the air, helped along by the sun and the rain. Not exactly what passersby on the street below ever would have expected.

13

Make your own...

You can uncover a leaf's skeleton in much the same way as you cleaned an animal's skeleton (see page 12). But it won't take as long and you won't get down to a skeleton of bones. Hold a leaf up to the light and you'll get a glimpse of what you will find — the leaf's food transport system of big and little veins. What do the veins do? They carry water that's full of nutrients to all the parts of the leaf. The water fills the leaf just as air fills and stiffens an air mattress. It holds the leaf up fresh and flat so that it can breathe and absorb sunlight.

You'll need:

- a flat watertight container (Plastic wrap held on with an elastic band makes a good lid.)
- tender thin leaves (They decay faster than tough thick leaves like oak.)
- 2 or 3 spoonfuls of fresh dirt (Soil from a garden or compost heap is rich in bacteria. It works best. Sterilized potting soil won't work at all.)
- water
- old newspapers

1. Put your leaves in the container and add enough water to cover them. Add the dirt to the water and stir gently.
2. Put the lid on the container and leave it for two weeks.
3. When you open the container it will smell of decay. Open it outside.
4. Test your leaves to see if they're ready for skeletonizing. Pick up a leaf and rub it gently

back and forth between your thumb and your index finger. It's ready when the top and bottom skin layers peel away from the middle layer in little rolls. If they don't, put the leaf back in your container and give the bacteria a little longer to work.

5. When a leaf is ready, lay it on the palm of your hand. Gently rub one outer skin layer off with your finger. Turn the leaf over and do the other side. Some kinds of leaves rip easily so be careful.

6. Dip the peeled middle layer in some fresh water. Rub it gently and help the water clean between the tiny veins. If the leaf feels tough enough, spray it with a gentle jet of water. Watch the leaf's gauzy skeleton come clean.
7. Leaf skeletons are delicate. Make them a little stronger by pressing and drying them. Lay them flat between two sheets of newspaper. Put a weight on top, such as a big heavy book or a stack of old newspapers. Leave them for three to four days or press and dry them the way museum botanists do (see the box on the next page).
8. Store the leaf skeletons flat or use them to decorate your room. Try gluing them onto a sheet of paper or taping them to your window.

Different kinds of leaves have different skeletons. How many can you uncover?

...leaf skeletons

MAKE A BOTANIST'S PRESS

1. Make a corrugated cardboard sandwich as shown. Be sure the corrugations of the cardboard run the same way.

2. Fasten a belt or rope around the outside as tightly as you can.

3. Set the press on its side in the sun for two or three days. Or hang it over a radiator. Make sure the corrugations are running up and down when you hang it, so the heat can flow through the press.

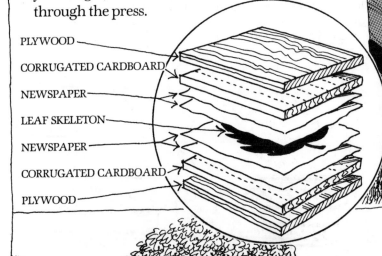

PLYWOOD
CORRUGATED CARDBOARD
NEWSPAPER
LEAF SKELETON
NEWSPAPER
CORRUGATED CARDBOARD
PLYWOOD

FOSSILIZED LEAVES

Leaves fell into rivers and swamps millions of years ago, just as they do today. Drifting dirt covered the leaves and piled up in heavy layers. The pressure of the dirt turned some buried leaves into stone. They became leaf fossils. Today botanists can study the leaf fossils to learn more about ancient plants and how they have evolved. By comparing the skeletons and tissue of ancient leaves with those of modern leaves, they can see how plants have changed or remained the same.

Make a pot pop

Picture a gleaming new car turning into a heap of rust before your eyes. Or your favourite new clothes growing thin and threadbare in an instant.

We don't expect objects to fall apart the moment they're made. But things do begin to rot, or "deteriorate," as soon as they come into contact with other things—like air or light or water. Fortunately, these changes usually happen slowly.

Archaeologists find many things people made long ago buried in the earth. But many of these artifacts have deteriorated so much that they're difficult to recognize. How does deterioration happen underground? Water from rain or snow seeps through the earth and picks up minerals from the soil. It soaks into things lying underground. As time passes, the ground—and whatever lies buried in it—dries out and gets wet over and over again. So what's the result? Try this experiment with one of the most common minerals in ground water—salt—and see what happens to a clay pot that gets wet and dries out again and again.

You'll need:

o *a plain red clay flower pot (unglazed)*
o *wax crayons*
o *a small jar or cup*
o *water*
o *table salt*
o *a shallow dish*

1. Decorate your clay pot with crayon. Press hard enough to make a bright design.

2. Fill the jar or cup with warm water. Add a heaping spoonful of salt. Stir or shake until the salt disappears. The salt is now dissolved in the water.

3. Set the pot in the shallow dish. Fill the dish with the salty water mixture.

4. Put your pot and dish somewhere warm. You might put it in the sun, near a radiator or in front of a fan, where the water will evaporate (and soak into the pot) quickly.

5. Let the water dry up. It will probably take a day or two. Add some more salty or plain water. Let the pot dry out and get wet over and over again. What happens to the pot? Keep on wetting and drying it for several weeks and you'll see pieces of the outside layer of the pot pop off.

Why does the pot pop? Look at a few grains of table salt with a magnifying glass. See the crystals? When salt is mixed with water, the crystals dissolve and take up less room. This salty water seeps into tiny holes in the pot. When the water dries up, the salt turns back into solid crystals that take up more room. The crystals push against the clay until — CRACK!—they pop the outer layer of clay right off the pot.

Why are some clay objects still in one piece when they're dug out of the ground? Probably because they were buried in a very dry place where salty ground water never touched them. Or in a very wet place where crystals never had a chance to form. A museum's problem comes when wet salt-soaked pots are dug up—and begin to dry out!

GO ON A ROT HUNT

Hints of rot are all around us. Here are a few to look for. Can you figure out what's causing the deterioration? Answers on page 96.

1. faded cloth
2. roofs turned green
3. blue-black patches on glue, leather, cloth or paper
4. brittle or yellowed paper
5. dull paint (look at old and new cars)
6. a white line on brick buildings, a bit above ground
7. metal that's turned rough and reddish brown

Bog bodies

Things rot so easily that it's amazing anything has lasted at all. But a quick glance around a museum will tell you that some things have lasted for thousands of years. They lasted because somehow they were protected.

You can see why the Danish farmers who discovered this body called the police. They thought they'd found the victim of a recent murder. In fact, this man died over 2000 years ago!

Tollund man was named after the place where he was found, a bog called Tollund Fen. A bog is a very old wetland where scrubby trees and low plants grow between pools of open water. Tollund man lasted because he was buried in a bog. Why? For two reasons.

First, bog water stands still. The oxygen in it was used up long ago. Without much oxygen, most bacteria can't live. And without bacteria, many things decay very slowly.

And second, although a bog doesn't have much oxygen, it does have a lot of tannic acid. That's the same acid that's in tea. This tea-like bath takes years to brew. It's made up of decaying bog plants. The bog water soaked into Tollund man and tanned him like leather. It made him a poor meal for the few insects and bacteria that lived in the bog.

The bog protected Tollund man well, right down to his fingernails and the short beard on his face. His brain and his inner organs were whole. Scientists were even able to take what was left of his last meal from his stomach and intestines. It was probably a thin porridge made from grains and seeds.

How did Tollund man end up in the bog? Scientists know he died a violent death because he was found with a leather noose around his neck. Perhaps he was a criminal. But more likely, he was killed as a sacrifice. Two thousand years ago, many Europeans believed in a goddess of the earth. They thought that unless they sacrificed a living person to her in the middle of the winter, spring would not come, crops would be poor and all the people would suffer.

MAKING THINGS LAST

What happens when you take something from the place where it's lasted for a long time? If conditions aren't right, some things can fall apart almost before your eyes. Museum conservators try to keep that from happening. They say that decay can't be stopped, but it can be slowed down.

How do conservators preserve bog bodies once they've been brought out of the bog into the air? The problem is to keep them from rotting or drying out. The earliest conservators tried smoking them like meat but that didn't work very well. Happily, modern-day conservators have found a way that does work—freeze-drying. It keeps bog bodies almost exactly as they were when they were dug up.

WATER PRESERVES AND WATER DESTROYS

Before people discovered how to make paper, they wrote on parchment. Parchment was made by stretching and scraping the skin of a sheep until it was dry, thin and flat. Sometimes there were holes in it but people just wrote around them. It was wonderfully tough. It could last for hundreds of years—unless it got wet. Then it wouldn't stay flat for long. It would start to curve back into its first sheepskin shape and get very hard. It would be badly damaged by the same wet conditions that keep a bog body safe.

What's wrong...

There's something odd about this picture. It's supposed to be a living room in the year 1850, but it's full of things that are in the wrong time. Things that are in the wrong time are called anachronisms (say a-na-crow-niz-ims). Spot ten of them and you'll have found them all. (Answers on page 96.)

Figuring out when things happened, when creatures lived and when things were made is important to museum scientists. It helps them tell the story of the earth and the plants and animals that have lived upon it. If they don't know when something happened or lived, the story gets muddled.

Over the last 100 years, scientists have developed more and more accurate ways of telling how old things are. That means it's getting easier to spot and fix a muddled story.

...with this picture?

The oldest parts of the earth that scientists have been able to date so far are rocks that formed about 3850 million years ago. Many scientists now think that the earth itself formed long before that, about 4600 million years ago.

Millions of years are impossible to imagine. But we can imagine time as a line like the one in the box. And we can set things on the line so that we can see how long they have been in this world. Compared to the dinosaurs or the oldest rocks, human beings haven't been around very long at all.

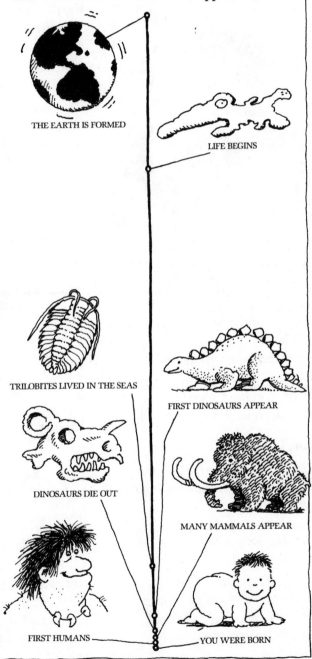

Imagine that this line represents the whole history of the earth. Look to see when the first dinosaurs and other creatures appeared on this time line. Notice how late humans appeared.

THE EARTH IS FORMED

LIFE BEGINS

TRILOBITES LIVED IN THE SEAS

FIRST DINOSAURS APPEAR

DINOSAURS DIE OUT

MANY MAMMALS APPEAR

FIRST HUMANS

YOU WERE BORN

Fake your own fossil

Fossils are the preserved remains of plants and animals that died long, long ago. Usually it takes millions of years for a fossil to form. You can't speed up time but you can fake your own fossil.

You'll need:

○ a small box like a shoe box
○ enough clay to make a layer 2 cm (¾ inch) thick in the bottom of the box (Play dough will work too but it won't make shapes as sharp as clay. See page 90 for the recipe.)
○ objects and tools for faking fossils—like twigs, leaves shells, nuts, screws and toothpicks

1. Most fossils formed under the floors of lakes and seas. To make your own lake or sea bed, work the clay with your hands until it's soft. Press it into the bottom and corners of the box. Smooth and shape your clay sea floor with your fingers or a spoon.

2. Plants and sea creatures died and sank to the bottom. Their soft parts decayed or were eaten by other creatures. Soon only their hard parts were left. To fake your own plant and animal remains, press objects into the clay to make imprints. Build up some raised shapes as well.

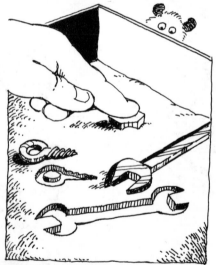

Congratulations. You've faked your own fossils. In real life, of course, a lot of time passed and many changes took place after plants and the bodies of animals sank to the bottom of lakes and seas.

A blanket of clay or silt settled quickly and gently over them. It protected them from decay and from hungry scavengers.

Layer after layer settled on top. The layers were heavy. They squashed the skeletons flat. After a long time, those layers turned to stone.

Water seeped through the stone and into the plant and animal remains. The water was full of minerals. Sometimes the minerals filled all the holes in the remains. Sometimes the water dissolved the remains till there was nothing left but a hole shaped exactly like the remains. Minerals often filled that hole and made a perfect stone copy of the remains. Fossils had formed.

At some time, the stony sea bed became dry land. Wind, ice and water wore away rock that protected the fossils.

Collectors spot some fossils but many are never discovered. They wear away like the rock around them.

REAL FOSSILS TO FAKE

Trilobites shed their outer skeletons as they grew. Many of these became fossils.

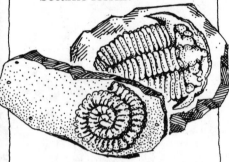

On the outside, ammonites look a lot like shells you can collect today. Most were quite small but some grew to be 3 m (3 yards) across.

Ancient worms left their traces on the sea floor. Birds left their footprints too.

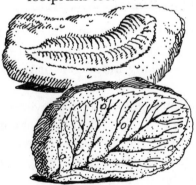

The soft parts of some leaves decayed. Only their veiny skeletons became fossils.

MAKE YOUR OWN FOSSIL CAST

You've probably packed a pail with wet sand and turned it over. The sand shape you made was a cast. It showed the exact shape of the pail.

Collectors sometimes make casts or copies of fossils. You can too, using plaster and the fossils you faked.

You'll need:

○ *plaster of Paris (page 91): how much you need depends on the size of your box*

1. Mix the plaster and pour it over your fake fossil while the clay or play dough is still wet. The plaster should be 4 cm (1½ inches) deep. Smooth the surface. You can mix and add more plaster if you don't have enough.

2. Let the plaster cool completely. When it's dry, rip and peel away the box.

3. Peel the clay away. If there's a lot of clay left on the plaster, hold the plaster under running water and clean it with an old toothbrush.

Special effects

- Sprinkle sand on the clay before pouring the plaster.
- Add any kind of paint to the plaster. Leave it in streaks or mix it in. Or fill your fossil imprints with coloured plaster and leave the rest white.
- Make the dried plaster look old. Sponge it with used, squeezed-out teabags.
- Make a small plaster cast and hang it on the wall. To do this, bend a paper clip to make a hanger. Stick it in the wet plaster.

Fossil-hunting tips...

Museum palaeontologists don't spend all their time in the museum. They also go out into the field to collect fossils. Read on to find out when and where they go fossil-hunting and how they bring fossils back to the museum. You can use some of their tips to find your own fossils.

Where to look

Fossils are found in rocks. But what kind of rocks? Although three basic kinds of rocks make up the earth's crust, most fossils are found in only one of them. Can you figure out which?

- Most *igneous* rock formed long ago when hot molten magma cooled and became the earth's crust. It still forms deep under the earth's surface. It pushes up into underground rock cracks and sometimes erupts from volcanoes.

- *Sedimentary* rock forms when bits of rock, soil or seashell settle onto the earth or sea-bottom. Layer after layer of these sediments build up and after a very long time, turn to stone.

- Most *metamorphic* rock forms when great heat or pressure inside the earth melts, bends or folds rock that's deep underground.

If you guessed that most fossils are formed in sedimentary rock, you're right. A fragile leaf or shell usually doesn't last long in igneous or metamorphic rock.

So if you go fossil-hunting, look for flat layers of sedimentary rock. You're likely to find them along the shores of lakes and rivers, along roads cut through rock or in quarries where stone or gravel has been taken from the ground.

Don't give up if you live where the land isn't flat. Sedimentary rock shows up in all sorts of landscapes. How come? Tremendous forces within the earth are always slowly moving the rocks of the earth's thin crust. For instance, the Burgess Shale is

...from the experts

- Sometimes you'll find an exciting bed of sedimentary rock on private property. Be sure to get permission to collect.
- If you do go to a quarry, stick to the quarry floor where there's no danger from loose, falling rock.
- Watch out for flying rock chips whenever you're using a hammer or chisel. Wear safety glasses and sturdy gloves

one of the best places in Canada for exceptional fossils. It was once a sea bed. Now it lies high on the slopes of the Rocky Mountains.

When to look

Spring is a good time to hunt for fossils. Winter rains, winds and snow have scoured the rocks and worn away their softest parts. Fossils that were hidden are now exposed.

How to look

If you find a thick slab of rock, look at its sides to see if it's in layers. If it is, you may be able to use a hammer and a chisel to split it open. Turn the slab on its side, fit your chisel along the edge of a layer and give it a good whack with your hammer. You never know what you'll find inside.

If you find a fossil in dark-coloured rock, breathe on it or wet it. The water or the moisture in your breath will darken it and help you see what's there.

If you find a fossil in super-hard rock, use an old toothbrush to loosen dry dirt or to scrub it under running water. A little dish-washing soap in water will finish the cleaning job when you get home.

Be sure to test your cleaning method (scrubbing under water, especially) on a corner or a piece that you don't mind losing.

Soft, moist or crumbly rock needs special care to keep it from falling apart. Wrap it in a damp paper towel and put it in a plastic bag. When you get home, treat it to make it stronger. Or treat it on the spot. First make a mixture of white glue and water (half and half). Then brush it over the rock, top and bottom—but not on the fossil itself. Let the mixture soak in and dry.

Keep your fossils from rubbing against one another in your pack. Wrap them in some paper towels or newspaper.

Solve a bony puzzle

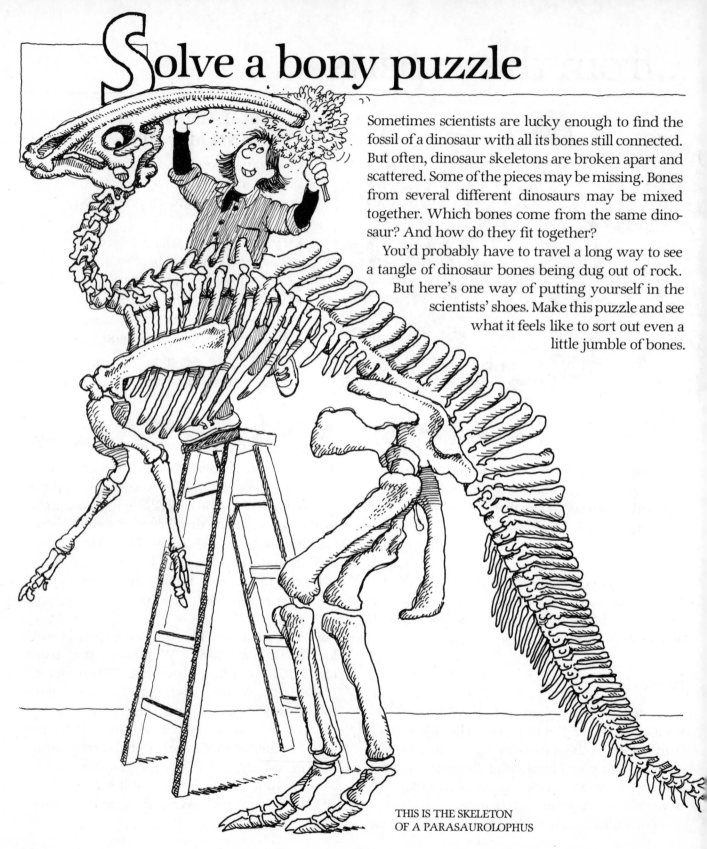

Sometimes scientists are lucky enough to find the fossil of a dinosaur with all its bones still connected. But often, dinosaur skeletons are broken apart and scattered. Some of the pieces may be missing. Bones from several different dinosaurs may be mixed together. Which bones come from the same dinosaur? And how do they fit together?

You'd probably have to travel a long way to see a tangle of dinosaur bones being dug out of rock. But here's one way of putting yourself in the scientists' shoes. Make this puzzle and see what it feels like to sort out even a little jumble of bones.

THIS IS THE SKELETON
OF A PARASAUROLOPHUS

You'll need:

o *a chicken wing*
  (raw or cooked)
o *a pot*
o *water*
o *kitchen tongs*
o *a sieve*

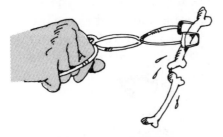

1. Put the wing in a pot. Cover it with water and bring the water to a boil. Turn down the heat and let the wing simmer for about 20 minutes or until the meat starts to fall off the bones.

2. Lift the wing out of the pot with tongs (ask an adult to help). If the wing is in pieces, collect them all by pouring everything through a sieve. Let it cool.

3. Pull the loose meat off the bones. (You may have to boil the bones again to get them completely clean.) Some very small bones are hidden inside soft gristle. To find them, peel away the gristle with your fingers. How many bones should you find? You should end up with 10 to 14 bones. The exact number depends on how old the chicken was. Why? A young chicken has little bones that aren't finished growing. As the chicken gets older, the little bones grow together and make larger single bones.

4. Spread out all your clean bones and see if you can figure out how they fit together. Not as easy as it looks? Imagine how much harder this puzzle would be if you didn't have all the pieces!

How can you tell when you've got it right? Scientists working with dinosaur bones don't always know that they're right. Since dinosaurs are extinct, scientists can't compare the way they've put a skeleton together with the real living thing. Unless an almost complete skeleton of the same kind of dinosaur has been discovered, all that scientists can do is make a best guess. Sometimes they're right—and sometimes they're wrong.

Fortunately chickens aren't extinct so you don't have to guess. Compare the way you put your wing together with the picture on page 96. Store your puzzle in a bottle or box. Why not let a friend try it?

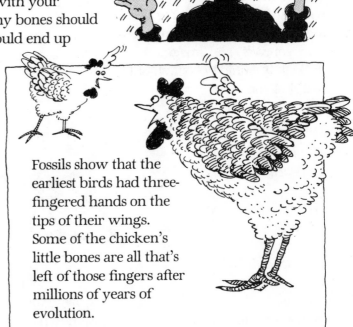

Fossils show that the earliest birds had three-fingered hands on the tips of their wings. Some of the chicken's little bones are all that's left of those fingers after millions of years of evolution.

Flesh out...

1. Put the paper over the Parasaurolophus skeleton on page 26 and trace around it. Just for now, ignore the arms and legs.

You've probably seen paintings or even life-sized models of dinosaurs. How do scientists know what dinosaurs looked like when all they usually have to go on is a pile of fossilized bones? Try fleshing out a cardboard dinosaur skeleton yourself, and imagine how difficult it would be to flesh out a real skeleton.

You'll need:

o *a piece of paper*
o *a pencil*
o *tape*
o *a piece of cardboard as big as these two pages*
o *scissors*
o *a teacup full of flour*
o *some water*
o *a bowl*
o *strips of newspaper about 2 cm (1 inch) wide*

2. Tape the tracing to the cardboard and cut around it to get your dinosaur's basic shape.

3. Cut out separate arms and legs. Use the skeleton as a guide, but make the legs a bit sturdier so your dinosaur will stand up.

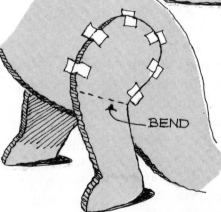

BEND

4. Bend these limbs out slightly as shown and tape them in place on the cardboard body.

5. If you think Parasaurolophus was fat, tape a ball of dry newspaper onto its stomach. Do the same to round the tail or limbs.

6. Put the flour in the bowl and mix in enough water to make a thick paste.

7. One by one dip the newspaper strips into the paste and wrap them around the cardboard dinosaur.

8. When you're satisfied with your Parasaurolophus' shape, let your skeleton dry, then paint it dinosaur colours.

Want to see what scientists think your dinosaur looks like? Turn to page 96.

...a dinosaur skeleton

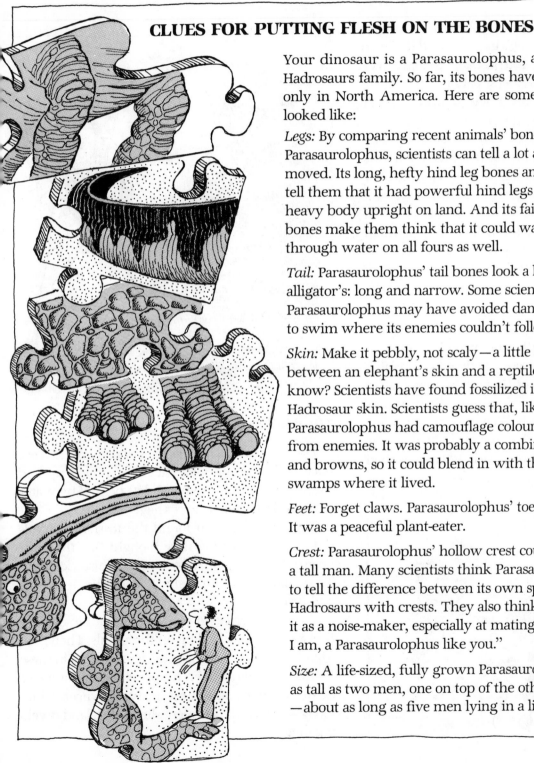

CLUES FOR PUTTING FLESH ON THE BONES

Your dinosaur is a Parasaurolophus, a member of the Hadrosaurs family. So far, its bones have been discovered only in North America. Here are some clues to what it looked like:

Legs: By comparing recent animals' bones with those of Parasaurolophus, scientists can tell a lot about how it moved. Its long, hefty hind leg bones and big hip bones tell them that it had powerful hind legs that could hold a heavy body upright on land. And its fairly long front leg bones make them think that it could walk or wade through water on all fours as well.

Tail: Parasaurolophus' tail bones look a lot like an alligator's: long and narrow. Some scientists think that Parasaurolophus may have avoided danger by using its tail to swim where its enemies couldn't follow.

Skin: Make it pebbly, not scaly—a little like a cross between an elephant's skin and a reptile's. How do we know? Scientists have found fossilized imprints of Hadrosaur skin. Scientists guess that, like animals today, Parasaurolophus had camouflage colours to help it hide from enemies. It was probably a combination of greens and browns, so it could blend in with the forests and swamps where it lived.

Feet: Forget claws. Parasaurolophus' toes ended in hoofs. It was a peaceful plant-eater.

Crest: Parasaurolophus' hollow crest could grow as long as a tall man. Many scientists think Parasaurolophus used it to tell the difference between its own species and other Hadrosaurs with crests. They also think the dinosaur used it as a noise-maker, especially at mating time, to say: "Here I am, a Parasaurolophus like you."

Size: A life-sized, fully grown Parasaurolophus would be as tall as two men, one on top of the other. But it was long —about as long as five men lying in a line.

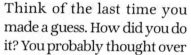ven best guesses...

Think of the last time you made a guess. How did you do it? You probably thought over what you knew about the situation, then made your guess. You probably knew that you didn't have all the facts, that you might be wrong.

Scientists often don't have all the facts and they don't wait until they do. Instead, they use what they know. They make the best guess they can and alter it as new facts are discovered. If scientists weren't willing to make best guesses and the mistakes that sometimes go along with them, it would take them much longer to figure things out. Of course, some best guesses turn out to be real bloopers.

Thumbs up!

Gideon Mantell knew this mean-looking spike belonged to a dinosaur that he named Iguanodon. But what part of the dinosaur's body was it? Mantell found only one spike, so he thought Iguanodon had a terrible weapon on its snout. But when miners found whole Iguanodon skeletons deep underground, scientists saw that the spike was in the wrong place. What's more, each Iguanodon had two spikes. They were really Iguanodon's thumbs. The plant-eater probably used them to slash and jab at its flesh-eating enemies.

The devil's corkscrew

These spirals are as deep as a very tall man and were once hollow. Long ago, they were filled up and made rock-hard by minerals left behind by water in the soil. But what were they?

The scientists who found the fossilized spirals didn't know. At first, they thought that they had been made by roots of a large prehistoric plant. They named the spirals Daimonelix — devil's corkscrew.

Two discoveries set things straight. First, scientists found rooms leading off the spirals. Then they found the fossil remains of ancient beavers in these rooms. The spirals weren't plant roots; they were beaver homes. But these beavers weren't like today's beavers. They were slim-tailed, land-dwelling diggers.

...can be wrong

Heads or tails?

Edward Drinker Cope and Othniel Charles Marsh were American experts on dinosaurs over a hundred years ago. Cope found the fossilized bones of a Plesiosaur, a sea-dwelling reptile that had a long, slim, bony neck and tail. He fitted the bones together, using his best guess, and showed the skeleton to Marsh. Cope's guess hadn't been good enough. Marsh saw that Cope had put the plesiosaur's head on its tail and said so.

Cope never forgave Marsh for pointing out his mistake. The two men became nasty rivals. Over the next 30 years, each tried to find more "new" dinosaur fossils than the other. Between them, they found about 130 different species!

Shrimp bits

About a hundred years ago, a geologist found a shrimp-like fossil in an ancient sea bed in the Rocky Mountains. One of the first scientists to study it named it Anomalocaris, which means "unlike other shrimps." He thought its head was missing.

Over the years, scientists found other fossils in the same ancient sea bed. What were they? Scientists weren't sure.

The mystery was finally solved when a scientist began cleaning what looked like just another shrimp-like Anomalocaris. To his surprise, as he chipped the rock away, he found more and more fossil. It turned out that the earlier fossils weren't separate animals; they were all parts of one big Anomalocaris. Scientists assembled the Anomalocaris like a jigsaw puzzle. When they had it all together, it was about half a metre (1½ feet) long. Compared with everything else living in the ancient seas, it was huge! It probably snatched up its prey with its shrimp-like limbs, opened its teeth outward and stuffed unfortunate trilobites in.

DISCOVER
the world around you

Lure some bugs, adopt a plant, make a sun-viewing box. Try out some new ways of looking and collecting that scientists use—and find out how much there is to see right at your doorstep. You won't have to go far to see some amazing sights.

Go out lighting

Unless you live in the country, you probably don't expect to see a bear or a deer feeding happily in your garden. But even in the heart of a city, you might be surprised at how many different insects make your neighbourhood their home.

To see many wild creatures, insects included, you have to know their habits. You have to seek them out where they live and feed. Try a method that museum entomologists use and learn a little about insects. Go out lighting and get the local insects to come to you.

A warm, dark summer night is the best time to go out lighting. If there's no moon or if it's cloudy, all the better. You'll have most success if you go out lighting near a garden.

You'll need:

○ *a strong light like a porch light or a movable light on an outdoor extension cord—a flashlight won't be bright enough*
○ *a white sheet*
○ *a lawn chair*
○ *tacks or clothespegs*

1. Turn on the porch light or hang the movable light so that it shines out towards the garden.

2. Hang the sheet so that the light shines on it. Stretch it out so that it hangs smoothly. You might tack the sheet to a wall or to a big tree trunk, drape it over a lawn chair or between two trees.

3. Turn off nearby lights. More insects will be attracted by your light if it's the only one around. Your light attracts nocturnal insects that rest during the day and are active at night.

4. Pull up a chair and watch as insects settle on the sheet. The light makes them think it's day and time to rest. They'll settle on dark surfaces like tree trunks too—only they'll be almost impossible for you to see.

5. When you've had enough, turn out the light. Then the insects will fly away.

6. If you have to go to bed before it gets dark, hang your sheet and your light out overnight and do your looking in the morning. Instead of stretching the sheet out smoothly, let it hang in loose folds. The insects will stay put all night because of the light. And the folds will give them somewhere to hide from hungry early-rising birds. Shake out your sheet when you've finished looking.

7. Some other things to do:

• Look up the insects that interest you most in a good field guide and find out what they are

• Keep a record every time you go out lighting; it helps to jot down what you saw and when and where.

AN UNUSUAL GARDEN

Who ever heard of a gardener planting weeds on purpose? Well, there is one. Bernard Jackson lives in Newfoundland and he's made a very unusual garden. It's for butterflies first and people second.

When you go out lighting, you lure insects that already live nearby. When you make a butterfly garden, you attract butterflies that haven't visited before. To do this, you have to give the butterflies just what they need. That's hard to do in Newfoundland, where it's often cold, wet and windy.

Wander through Jackson's garden and you'll see logs stacked like little cabins to give adult butterflies shelter from the wind and the cold. Wide paths through the forest give them sun and open spaces. Ordinary garden flowers and weeds like nettles and dandelions give leafy food to newly hatched larvae and nectar to full-grown butterflies.

How do Jackson and his gardeners know what butterflies like? It's simple. They watch the 26 kinds of butterfly that now visit the garden. They notice what they eat, where they lay their eggs and where they go for shelter.

Flowering carrots?

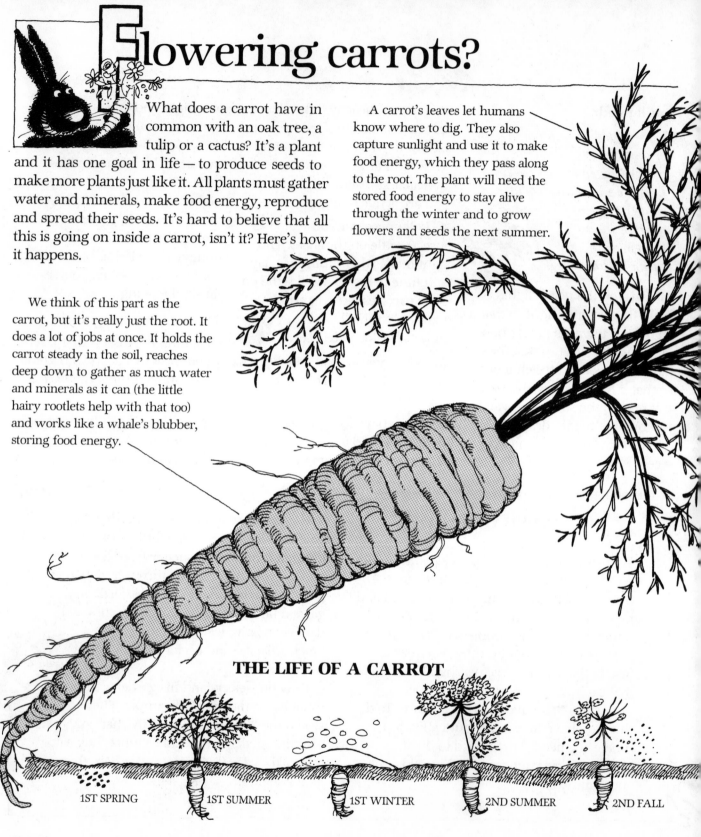

What does a carrot have in common with an oak tree, a tulip or a cactus? It's a plant and it has one goal in life — to produce seeds to make more plants just like it. All plants must gather water and minerals, make food energy, reproduce and spread their seeds. It's hard to believe that all this is going on inside a carrot, isn't it? Here's how it happens.

A carrot's leaves let humans know where to dig. They also capture sunlight and use it to make food energy, which they pass along to the root. The plant will need the stored food energy to stay alive through the winter and to grow flowers and seeds the next summer.

We think of this part as the carrot, but it's really just the root. It does a lot of jobs at once. It holds the carrot steady in the soil, reaches deep down to gather as much water and minerals as it can (the little hairy rootlets help with that too) and works like a whale's blubber, storing food energy.

THE LIFE OF A CARROT

1ST SPRING   1ST SUMMER   1ST WINTER   2ND SUMMER   2ND FALL

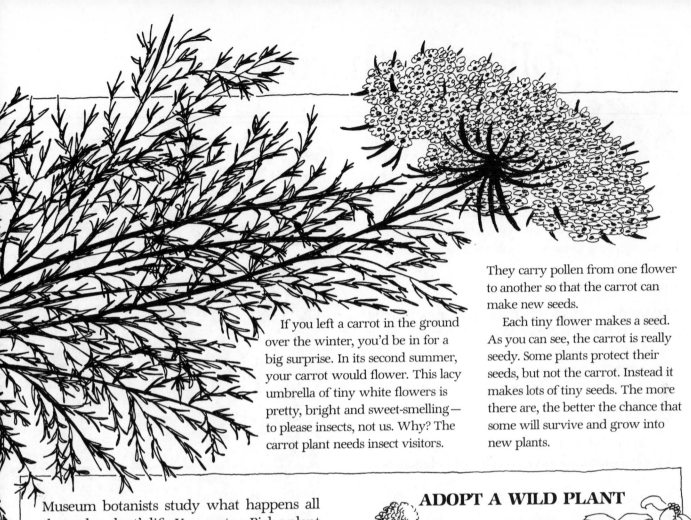

If you left a carrot in the ground over the winter, you'd be in for a big surprise. In its second summer, your carrot would flower. This lacy umbrella of tiny white flowers is pretty, bright and sweet-smelling— to please insects, not us. Why? The carrot plant needs insect visitors.

They carry pollen from one flower to another so that the carrot can make new seeds.

Each tiny flower makes a seed. As you can see, the carrot is really seedy. Some plants protect their seeds, but not the carrot. Instead it makes lots of tiny seeds. The more there are, the better the chance that some will survive and grow into new plants.

Museum botanists study what happens all through a plant's life. You can too. Pick a plant that you want to get to know—maybe a tree, bush, weed, wild flower or garden flower. They are all plants: they all have roots, leaves, stems, flowers and seeds.

Tie a strip of plastic bag or a twist tie around your plant's stem so you can find it again. Visit it often. Each time, try to notice something you've never noticed before. Nothing about a plant is accidental. Everything has a purpose. Look at how its parts are shaped and arranged. Watch how it changes as the seasons go by. You don't need more than your eyes, but a magnifying glass, a camera or a notebook and pencil make looking even more fun.

ADOPT A WILD PLANT

Collect with your eyes...

Walk into a field or woods and the birds and animals will probably know that you're coming. They're wary of people and will keep out of your way. If you want to see them, you'll have to show them that you don't mean danger. Follow these tips from museum zoologists and learn more about where and how to look for animals.

Know where to look

- Edges make great watching spots, especially at dusk. What's an edge? Wherever one kind of landscape meets another—for example, where a field meets a forest, a road or a river—you get an edge. Where the two kinds of landscape meet, so do the creatures that live in them. When you sit in a field, you'll see the creatures of the field. But when you sit in the narrow band of land where the field meets the forest, you'll see field and forest creatures.

- Because many different animals gather at edges, hunting animals often prowl there. You may be lucky and see one of them.

- Shorelines where animals come to drink are good edges to watch. Often you can see animal pathways leading to the water. Look for telltale openings in the underbrush and tracks on wet sand or mud.

Become as silent and invisible as you can

- Find a comfortable place to sit. Then wait quietly. Be as still as you can. After about 10 or 15 minutes, the field or forest may well come alive around you.

- Animals often have a very keen sense of smell. So do mosquitoes! They will know you by your own human scent. Don't make your presence even more obvious by washing with perfumed soap.

...and your ears

Try a different way of looking

- Look straight ahead at one thing and keep looking at it. At the same time, concentrate on noticing as much as you can around you without actually looking sideways. Look for movement. You can practise this anywhere, even at the supper table. Keep staring at something on the table. Without moving your eyes, notice as much as you can about what's happening around the table.

- Once you see something move, look right at it. If it's far away, look at it through binoculars or wait till it comes closer. If you move suddenly, you'll scare most animals away. To an animal, movement often means that a hunter is attacking.

Listen closely

It's very noisy in the woods. Try to tell bird and animal sounds from other noises. They are clues to animals' movements. Can you sort out the different sounds you hear? Listen for trees creaking in the wind, leaves rustling, insects chirping and whirring, birds calling or hopping up and down tree trunks and animals rustling among grasses, leaves or twigs.

Uncover small worlds

Many of the smallest creatures won't be out in the open. Lift a log or a stone and you'll probably find a colony of tiny bugs, beetles or worms. Lift the log gently—and remember to put it back the way you found it. If you don't, you'll have changed the colony's sheltered climate. It's a little like plunging a warm town full of people into icy weather and leaving them to survive if they can.

Remember what zoologists say: some days you won't see a lot. Don't give up. Other days, you'll spot one bird or animal after another.

Watch the sun...

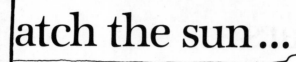

Today, astronomers use powerful telescopes to study the universe. But like people in the past, you can learn a lot just by looking with your eyes. There's only one star you shouldn't stare at—the sun. It's much closer to us than any other star. Its light is still very strong when it reaches the earth. Look directly at it and you could really damage your eyes. But there is a safe way to watch the sun. Make a sun-viewing box!

You'll need:

- two large cardboard boxes that, when set end to end, are at least 30 cm (12 inches) high by 60 cm (24 inches) long
- a sharp knife or good scissors
- gray duct tape
- 4 sheets of white paper
- black paper big enough to cover the two boxes
- aluminum foil
- a pin
- an old head scarf

1. Cut one end out of each box as shown.

2. Cover the inside end of one box with sheets of white paper. This will be the screen on which you will see the sun's image.

3. Cover the rest of the inside of the boxes with black paper. The darker it is inside your sun-viewing box, the brighter the image will look on the white screen.

4. Tape the two boxes together as shown to make one long box. It must be at least 60 cm long, but it can be longer.

5. Tape over any holes so that no light can leak in. Be sure to cover all the corners and the places where the flaps meet.

6. Cut a hole just big enough for your head in the bottom of the box. Put the hole towards the black end of the box, not towards the white end.

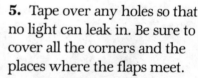

...but don't look at it

7. Cut a small hole about 8 cm × 8 cm (3 inches × 3 inches) in the end opposite the white screen. The hole must be higher than your head when the box rests on your shoulders.

8. Cut a piece of aluminum foil that's a little bigger than the hole. Tape it over the hole on the outside of the box. Tape all around the edges so no light can slip in.

9. Use the pin to make a tiny hole in the centre of the aluminum foil.

10. Put the box over your head. Wrap the scarf around your neck to keep out light.

11. Bend over as shown. Aim the white screen at your feet and the pinhole at the sun. Look at the screen. Expect to see a small image of the sun!

Your sun-viewing box is perfect for watching solar eclipses safely. They don't happen often but they're exciting when they do. They happen when the moon passes between the earth and the sun. The moon blocks the sun's light and casts a shadow on the earth. That means it gets quite dark in the middle of the day.

Experiment with your viewing box:

- Aim the pinhole at other things. Make sure that the sun or a bright sky is behind them.
- Use your box without bending over. What happens to the image on the screen?
- Try using longer boxes. Does the sun's image change?
- Try different sizes and patterns of pinholes. Use several pieces of foil.

41

Hunt for the riches...

phone

cotton sweatshirt

pet cage

sneakers

comics

Long ago, people discovered that stone made good weapons and tools. They found that clay made good pots. People have been using the riches of the earth ever since. As time has passed, we have used more and more of them. Our ancient ancestors would be amazed if they could see all the different materials we take from the earth and how we use them. So would our great-grandparents.

Just how much do we depend on the earth today? Take a good look around this room and see for yourself. Try to guess which of the labelled objects come from the earth and which don't. Then turn to page 96 to see how you did.

How can you tell what comes from the earth? Look for things that are made from oil, rocks and minerals. The only problem is that it's often hard to tell what something is made of. These clues will help:

- Oil usually starts out as a thick liquid but don't be fooled by that. It's used to make plastics, synthetic cloth like polyester, linoleum and many paints.

...of the earth

light
mirror
desk
aquarium
Walkman
paints
piggy bank

- Look for rock that has been broken down by wind, water or ice into smaller and smaller bits until it becomes sand or clay. They are used in glass, pottery, china, ceramics, bricks and concrete.
- Rocks are made up of minerals. Some minerals are metallic (like gold) but others aren't (like salt and talc). Watch for silver, copper, iron, graphite (pencil leads) and anything that looks metallic.

The riches or resources that we use come from the earth's crust. The crust isn't very deep, usually only

35 to 40 km (22 to 25 miles) deep. At most it's 70 km (44 miles) thick. It's a thin coating on the earth, like an apple's peel. Geologists study the earth to find out how it formed and where we can find useful rocks, minerals and oils. They have discovered that it took a very long time for those resources to form. The minerals and rocks can be used over and over again but the oils and the plastics made from oil can't. If we're smart, say the geologists, we'll take from the earth with care and without waste and we'll re-use what we can.

Underwater clues...

Have you ever lost something and, while looking for it, found something else that you'd lost long ago? If so, you've experienced serendipity: you've made a happy but unexpected discovery. Serendipity helped museum scientists make a major discovery at Crawford Lake in Ontario.

Crawford Lake is a small, deep lake west of Toronto. Lakes of this kind, called "meromictic lakes," are found all over the world. But they are rare and of special interest to many scientists. Why?

In most lakes, all the water mixes together and churns up the mud on the bottom. In meromictic lakes, the water is so deep that it doesn't get disturbed. Things that fall into the lake sink to the bottom, pile up and stay there for thousands of years in layers that you can see. Because of this, palaeobotanists (scientists who study fossilized plants) can take samples of bottom mud and find out about the plants that lived on the shores of the lake long ago.

That's just what was happening at Crawford Lake in 1971. A palaeobotanist decided to collect a sample of bottom mud in order to study the pollen grains it contained. By looking at the fossilized pollen in the lake mud, he hoped to learn what plants had grown near the lake for hundreds of years and how they had changed.

To collect bottom mud, the botanist filled a heavy hollow tube with dry ice to make it freezing cold. He lowered this "frigid finger" into the lake and into the mud. When he pulled it up ten minutes later, it was coated with a thin crust of frozen mud.

Back at the lab, the botanist and his assistant studied the frozen crust. They could see layers, two for each year. The top two layers were from 1971. The further down they went, the older the layers and the pollen were. They studied the pollen from dif-

...to a buried village

How do you find the remains of a settlement that disappeared long ago? If you're an archaeologist, you look for signs that people have somehow changed the land—telltale ridges or bumps or hollows. You watch for artifacts dug up by groundhogs or by a farmer's plough. And you go to people who know the land better than you do—like farmers.

It turned out that the farmer who had lived on the shores of Crawford Lake had collected a basketful of stone axes and arrowheads on his land. He'd found most of them in his barnyard. Sure enough, when archaeologists dug up the barnyard, they found pottery, food storage pits, stains from old firepits and marks in the earth from long house posts. And in the garbage pits, they found charred kernels of corn! The botanist's guess was right. Native people had once lived on the shores of the lake and had grown corn.

So, the botanist learned what he'd set out to learn: how the forest around the lake had changed. In the process he found clues to a buried village and, thanks to the corn pollen, he could tell when people had lived there. The archaeologist took over and uncovered the village. He owed his find to serendipity.

ferent years to see what kinds of plants had grown around the lake.

Then they found something unusual. The mud layers that were about 530 years old were loaded with corn pollen. At first the botanist didn't believe it. Why would corn pollen suddenly show up in the middle of a forest? Had native people lived on the shores of the lake, cut down the trees and planted corn fields? The botanist went to an archaeologist for help.

45

DISCOVER

clues to the past

What can you learn from a mound of earth, a piece of broken pot or an ancient grave? Lots. Find out how scientists look for clues as they try to solve the mysteries of past civilizations. Puzzle over some curious artifacts. Then put yourself in an archaeologist's shoes—thousands of years in the future—and try to imagine what he or she might think of us.

# Melting houses

Mounds of earth don't grow, do they? Well, this one did. When people first lived here, there was no mound. But over 4000 years—as they threw out their garbage, abandoned old homes and built new ones — the mound grew slowly, layer upon layer.

To archaeologists today, the mound is a record of the past. The further down they dig, the further back they go in time. Each layer has its own story to tell. If you could take a close-up look at the layers of this mound, here's what you could find out.

3. About 4400 years ago: Earthquake! Roofs caved Houses collapsed. People fled taking only what they could carry. They left many things behind the ruins. Twenty years later, the ruined house had melted too. Whatever was left inside them was buried. The mound grew.

2. About 5200 ago: This isn't just dirt. It's what you find after houses made of mud brick melt back into the earth. Mud bricks are easy and cheap to make but they only last about forty years. Then, it's easier to build a new house than to repair the old one. People took the old roof beams with them because wood was scarce. A melted house added up to a metre of earth to the top of the mound.

1. About 5800 years ago: Does this look like garbage to you? It should. It's garbage left by the first people who ever lived here. They dug pits in the mud and threw in their garbage. They used the mud they dug out to make bricks for their houses.

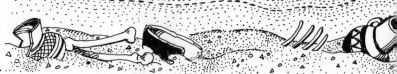

5. About 2300 years ago: The village flourished . . . until the wells started to dry up. Without water, people couldn't survive. So they left the mound for the last time and searched for a new place to live.

4. About 3800 years ago: People rebuilt the village. It was a good place to live. The soil was rich. There was plenty of fresh water. And it was close to trade routes. Other tribes saw how wealthy the new village had become. One night, they attacked. They set fires and damaged the homes. The survivors tore down the ruined houses, levelled the land and built new homes. The mound grew.

DIGGING DEEP

A real mound that grew up over 4000 years would have many more layers than this one does. The Godin Tepe mound in Western Asia grew higher than an 8-storey building.

Digging destroys ancient evidence, so archaeologists work very carefully. They use everything from toothbrushes and dental picks to shovels. When they find something, they record everything they can about where they found it and what else was nearby. If they don't, clues to the past will be lost forever.

ot puzzlers

Dream of being an archaeologist and maybe you dream of finding a buried city or an ancient tomb laden with magnificent treasures. Archaeologists do make extraordinary finds but, in between, they find many more ordinary clues to the past, clues like pieces of broken everyday pottery. A potsherd (a piece of pottery) may sound boring, but if you fit a heap of sherds together, sometimes you get a whole pot. Here's a pot puzzle to try yourself.

You'll need:

- a pot or bowl made of clay or china that you have been given permission to break
- a heavy paper bag
- a hammer
- white glue and a brush
- masking tape
- plaster of Paris or filling compound
- fine sandpaper (optional)
- acrylic paints and a brush (optional)

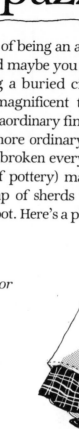

1. Put the bowl or pot inside the bag and break it by whacking it a few times with a hammer. Don't overdo it or you'll get a lot of very small pieces and a very difficult puzzle.

2. Archaeologists don't often find a whole pot. To make your puzzle more like the real thing, remove two or three sherds.

3. Sort the rest of the potsherds into piles: pieces from the base of the pot, pieces from the rim, pieces from the middle.

4. Start with the bottom of the pot. When you find two pieces that fit together, brush a thin coat of glue on the edges that meet. Press them together. Stretch a piece of tape across the break as shown to hold the pieces together.

5. Set the glued pieces aside for 30 minutes to let the glue harden. Glue and tape other pieces together as you wait. Piece by piece you'll put your whole pot together.

6. Let the glue dry overnight, then remove the tape.

7. You'll see some holes from the missing pot sherds. Inside the pot, stick masking tape over each hole.

8. Mix up a little plaster of Paris or filling compound. On the outside of the pot, fill in the holes you just taped. Let the

HOW MUCH CAN A PIECE OF POT TELL YOU?

These pots were made by the Maya people of Central America. The youngest was made about 1200 years ago, the oldest about 2400 years ago. They show that the Maya developed new skills and learned new ways of making and decorating their pots. the youngest? the oldest? (Answer on page 96.)

Archaeologists try to match a pot style with a time, a place and a people. Then, if they find the same style of pot again, they can be pretty sure about who made it, where and when.

patches dry and then smooth with fine sandpaper. If you want, you can paint the patches.

Ready for more of a challenge? Get a friend to put a pot you've never seen into the bag. Or two or three different pots. Then tackle a tricky sorting job.

One sherd can be confusing. A narrow base might be part of a narrow pot. But then again, it might spread out like the pot on the right.

When archaeologists find a large part or all of a pot, it's much less confusing.

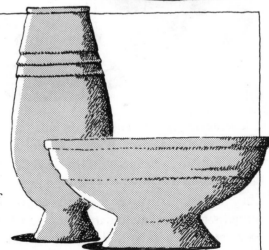

Send a message...

You can't take it with you. Or can you? People have always wondered what happens after death. Does everything end? Is there life after death? If there is, what's it like? Do the dead need things from this life in the afterlife?

Sometimes when archaeologists are digging on a site, they find a grave in which the dead have been buried with things to help them in the next life. For archaeologists, this is like finding a time capsule. Things that are found in graves aren't there by accident. They were put there on purpose. They help archaeologists build up a picture of what life was like for one person at one time.

What did people long ago put in their graves? What do those things tell us today?

Mini-dishes

These dishes are miniature versions of the dishes the Etruscans (ancient Italian people) used every day. They buried them with the dead because they believed that the dead needed food in the afterlife. They buried many other everyday things they thought the dead would need too, such as food, cooking pots, combs and mirrors, brooches and necklaces, weapons and armour.

Soul houses

Ancient Egyptians who couldn't afford grand tombs made small model houses to mark their graves instead. These soul houses looked very much like real houses. They even had stairs up to the roof. (In real houses people slept on rooftops on hot nights.) Some archaeologists think that a soul house, along with the grave below, was meant to give the soul a home. And in its small open courtyard, the living could leave food, oil and water for the dead.

...to the future

A rich grave

This Maya ruler-priest was buried with rich grave goods. Archaeologists found his tomb near the top of a temple of the sun god. He must have been a powerful and much-respected person because he was the only ruler-priest in the temple to be buried with the head of Kinich Ahau, the sun god. The head was carved from a piece of precious green jade about the size of a small cantaloupe. It was a treasured symbol to the Maya. Yet they decided to bury it forever.

MAKE A TIME CAPSULE THAT LASTS

What would you put in a time capsule of your own? Maybe you would want to draw a picture or tape record familiar sounds and voices. Or you could collect objects that say something about your time or take photographs (use black-and-white film; it'll last longer). Now you'll need a container and a safe place to store it. Should it be something airtight and buried underground? Nope.

1. Use an ordinary box and line it with high-quality paper so that acid in the box paper won't damage what's inside. Because it's not airtight, it won't trap moisture. That means mould and decay won't start.
2. Wrap the things to go in your capsule with high-quality paper. This will prevent different materials from damaging one another. For example, the copper of a penny will stain a newspaper if they touch for a long time.

3. Label each thing with an HB pencil. Pencil is better than any pen. It won't fade or run.
4. Close the box to protect the contents from dust and light—but don't seal it.
5. Store it away from heat and dampness—in other words, not in a basement or attic. Wait for at least 10 years before opening it!

The best kind of paper to use is acid-free (found in art supply stores). But any good paper will do.

What on earth are these?

When you see a museum artifact all by itself, it's easy to forget that somebody made it and somebody used it. It was part of someone's life, the way your shoes or your bike or your sunglasses are part of yours. In fact, many artifacts (including the ones on this page) helped people solve problems. The question is—what problems?

Look at each of these artifacts and ask yourself: what problem was the inventor trying to solve when he or she invented this? Did he need to do something he'd never done before? Or did she get so peeved with something that didn't work that she sat down and thought up something new? The experts don't always know what an artifact is right away. Don't be disappointed if you don't either. When you've made the best guess you can, turn the page to find out the real story—at least, as far as we know it.

1. This cluster of brightly coloured, golf-ball-sized pompoms was collected from the Guahiro people. They live in a hot, dry part of South America where sand dunes run all along the sea coast. What do they use the pompoms for?

2. This hard ceramic artifact is hollow and about the size of a large round loaf of bread. Archaeologists found artifacts like this when they excavated ancient Chinese houses, especially the sleeping quarters. What is it?

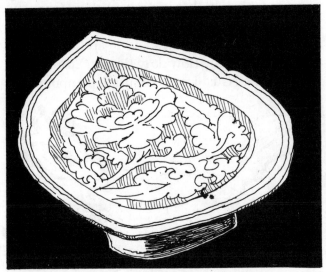

3. The bark has been stripped off this bent piece of twig, which is about the size of your hand. It was collected in 1953 from people living in West Africa. Want a clue? The shredded end is stiff.

4. Artifacts like these come in pairs. These were collected in Alaska early this century. Each one is about the size of a mouth organ. They are made of ivory, probably from the tusks of walruses. Notice the pointy nubs carved on the bottom. What are these artifacts and how were they used?

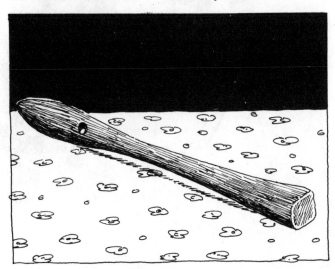

5. No one knows exactly where or when this finger-sized Egyptian artifact was collected or if anything else was found nearby. It's made of wood and was carved smooth. What could it be?

55

Ahh...so *that's* what they are

Now that you've made your best guesses about the artifacts on the previous page, here's what the experts really do and don't know about them.

1. Tie a cluster of pompoms to a small precious thing and it won't get lost in the sand. The pompoms are so bright that you can see them far away. And they are so light that they spread out on the sand like little parachutes and keep things from sinking out of sight. How do we know? Ethnologists have watched Guahiro people using pompoms this way.

2. This rock-hard object is a pillow or head rest. How do we know? People in China wrote about hard pillows long ago and still know about them today. Some head rests even have the Chinese word for 'pillow' written on them. Believe it or not, some modern doctors think that hard pillows are better for your neck than soft pillows.

ZZZZZZ ZZZZZz

3. This toothbrush has bristles that wear out faster than plastic ones—but cut off the tips and the brush is as good as new. How do we know? The person who collected this toothbrush probably saw people making and using toothbrushes just like it.

4. The Inuit strapped these ice cleats onto their boots or mukluks. The cleats made it possible to walk on slick ice or snow. The points dug in and gave the walker traction. How do we know? Early scientific expeditions to the Arctic recorded many details about the land and the people. And many Inuit today still know what the cleats are and how they were used.

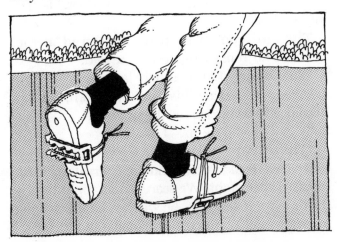

5. Were you stumped by this one? So were the experts. Now they think that they may have stumbled on the answer. How? A hairdresser came to the museum to make Egyptian-style wigs. He used modern perming curlers. They looked very familiar. In fact, they looked very much like this puzzling artifact. Was it really a curler? Only new evidence—such as an ancient wig with curlers in it—will give sure proof.

Collect scary stories...

Almost everybody likes a scary story, whether it's true or not. Have you heard these two before?

An old man lived all by himself in a cottage in the woods. Every night he would do the same thing: carefully lock all the doors and windows and then turn out the lights. One night, after the last light was out, he heard a voice behind him say, "Good — we're locked in for the night."

If that story doesn't make the hair on the back of your neck stand on end, try this one. It was told by a young man who claimed it really happened to him. Here's what he said:

One Hallowe'en night, as I was driving home from a party, I saw a guy about my age standing at the corner of Maple and Victoria Streets, hitchhiking. I stopped and offered him a lift. His clothes looked old fashioned and not very warm. He didn't have a jacket. The night was chilly and he was shivering. So I said, "There's an extra sweater in the back. You can wear it if you want." "Thanks," he said and pulled it on over his head.

It turned out that he lived quite close to my place. We talked and joked and, as I pulled up in front of his place, we agreed to get together the next day. He got out, grinned, went up the driveway and disappeared behind the house. Suddenly I realized he hadn't given me back my sweater — but I thought, "It's okay, I'll get it back tomorrow."

So the next day, I went back to my new friend's house. An old woman answered the door. "Is Tom in?" I asked.

The old woman gasped and stared at me. "There's no Tom living here," she said.

"But I dropped him off here last night."

"We had a son and his name was Tom, but he's been dead and buried for thirty years."

"What do you mean?" I asked.

"Thirty years ago last night, he went to a Hallowe'en party. He didn't come home. There was a freak blizzard that night. We searched all night but by the time we found him, he was dead. He was lying in a snowbank at the corner of Maple and Victoria."

...and real-life stories

"I don't believe it," I said. "I just drove him home last night!"

"You can visit his grave yourself," said his old mother.

I got back in the car and drove straight to the cemetery. There were lots of leaves on the ground and they had piled up against the gravestones. It took me a while to find Tom's grave—but at last I found it. I reached down to brush the leaves away. Suddenly something familiar caught my eye. There, part in and part out of the ground, was my sweater!

COLLECT A TRUE STORY

There are lots of made-up stories—and lots of versions of them. For example, scholars have collected more than 700 versions of Cinderella.

There are also true stories that people have passed along. Anthropologists and historians visit people who remember what life was like in different times and places and collect their stories about everyday life and important events. The scholars use these memories just as they use pots and other artifacts—to build a picture of times and places that are changing or gone.

You can collect made-up or true stories. Use a tape recorder or listen carefully. Parents, grandparents and adult friends are good sources of true stories. Try asking them about:

- what it was like when they were young and what changes they have seen
- what scares and adventures they have had
- how they came to this country (if they came from someplace else).

Archaeologists...

Suppose archaeologists discovered your bathroom 10 000 years from now. By then, people will probably live very differently from the way we live now. They may not even have bathrooms. Imagine how puzzled they will be at the things they find in your bathroom.

If archaeologists haven't seen things in use, they have to take a guess at what they are. As we have already seen, some best guesses can go wrong (see page 30). Once one bad guess is made, others often follow. What would happen if future archaeologists made the mistake of thinking your bathroom was a whole house, instead of just one room?

Probably a sleeping surface. The lack of an air cushion and heat cover makes it look hard, cold and uncomfortable by our standards. Some experts think that some sort of soft material may have flowed onto the surface through the nozzle at one end.

This seems to have been a space divider, separating the living space from the sleeping space. Notice the fish symbols. These have been found on many objects. Fish may have been a major food or perhaps these people worshipped them.

At first experts thought that this was a container for the fish that were so important to these people. Now they believe that it was a small hydroponic garden, part of the home's food supply.

...of the future

A most puzzling object. It seems to be a smaller version of the large sleeping space. Some experts suggest that it was used for infants. (The exit hole in the bottom may have been a clever way of removing infant wastes. Why the larger sleeping space has a similar hole remains a mystery.)

This was probably the home's food bank. Like us, these people seem to have condensed their food and stored it in tubes and pills. Some of the contents have survived, although they are completely dried out. Once these contents are analysed, we will have some idea of what these people ate.

The uses of the other objects discovered in this dwelling are still unknown. What do you think they were used for?

In all these artifacts, stiff bristles are set into a hard substance. Because these artifacts are so similar, experts believe that they were used for the same purpose. Could they have been used by people of different sizes? For cleaning their teeth? their backs?

This headdress is very fragile though the fish images can still be seen. Perhaps it was worn for special ceremonies in the home.

DISCOVER

ways of stepping back in time

Ever wanted to make yourself a knight's plumed helmet or some magnificent beads, to challenge a friend to a game that the ancient Egyptians enjoyed or to share a meal, medieval-style? In this chapter, you'll find out how. You'll also learn how ancient peoples solved basic problems— like keeping warm, protecting themselves and preparing food. Try solving the same problems yourself.

Make your own loom

The clothes you're wearing right now were probably woven on a huge mechanical loom. But for thousands of years, people wove beautiful cloth by hand on very simple looms. Many people still weave on hand looms today.

As long as you've got two points for fastening and stretching the lengthwise warp threads, you've got a loom. No matter what loom you use, the basic idea of weaving is simple and stays the same. Get ready to weave . . . and discover the basic idea for yourself.

You'll need:

- *a shoebox lid*
- *a sharp knife*
- *a ball of yarn*
- *stiff cardboard*
- *scissors*
- *an afro pick or a comb with widely spaced teeth*
- *two sticks, each a little longer than the lid is wide*

Make a loom

1. Use the knife to cut slots along both ends of the lid. The slots should be about 1 cm (½ inch) deep and 1 cm (½ inch) apart. Make the same number of slots at either end.

2. Tie a knot about 10 cm (4 inches) from the free end of the ball of yarn. Slip the knot and its tail into one of the end slots.

3. String the yarn back and forth in an S-pattern as shown until you reach the last slot. The yarn should not hang loosely or pull in too tightly.

4. Knot the yarn snugly against the outside of the last slot and cut off the end. Now you've stretched your warp threads on your loom.

Make a shuttle

1. Cut a rectangle of stiff cardboard about 10 cm by 4 cm (4 inches by 1½ inches).
2. Cut a V in either end. Round off the pointy tips.
3. Wind some yarn onto your cardboard. Now you've got a shuttle of yarn.

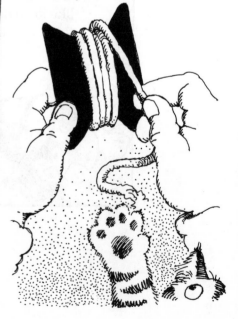

Weave a wall hanging

1. Unwind some yarn from the shuttle. Guide the shuttle over the first warp thread, under the next—and over and under until you reach the far side. You'll tuck in the loose end after you come back the other way.

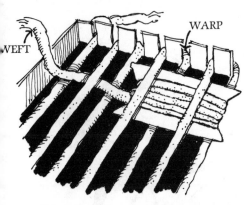

2. Start back across the other way. If your first crosswise, or "weft," thread went under the last warp thread, start this one by going over it. If it went over, start by going under.

3. Before you start the third weft thread, weave the loose end in with your fingers.

4. Don't pull the yarn tight as you weave. Every time you get to the far side, tug gently till the looseness is gone. Then use the pick or comb or a pencil to push the weft thread you've just woven against the ones you've done already.

5. When you run out of yarn, use your fingers to weave the loose end in—over and under about 4 warp threads. Wind more yarn onto the shuttle. Start it in the same way you started the first shuttle (step 1).

6. Weave as close as you can to the end of the lid. When the shuttle won't fit, use your fingers to weave as close as you can to the end.

7. Get the two sticks ready for taking your weaving off the loom. Lift the loops of warp thread out of the end slots one at a time, starting at the end without the knot. Slip each loop onto a stick as you go. When you reach the knotted end, tie the knot's tail around the stick.

You can make a whole hanging out of one colour of yarn—but you don't have to. You can weave anything you want in and out of the warp threads. Try other colours and sizes of yarn, twisted plastic wrap, interesting grasses or sticks, tufts of raw wool, twists of cloth, strips of bright felt. Tuck the ends in or leave them ragged.

Dye by trial and error

When you reach into your cupboard, you can probably pull out clothes of many colours. Where do the colours come from? About 120 years ago, scientists discovered how to mix chemicals to make dyes that stay bright and are easy to use. But for thousands of years before that, skilful dyers coaxed colour out of plants, insects and shellfish. Bright colours were often rare and costly, worn only by the rich.

In those days, dyers knew how to make many beautiful colours but dyeing was hard, smelly work. The dye wouldn't stay in the cloth without special preparations. Figuring out how to do this well took a lot of experimenting. In many places, dyers kept their recipes secret.

Try experimenting with some homemade dyes and see what colours you end up with.

You'll need:

o *newspapers*
o *a big non-metal or coated metal pot*
o *water*
o *an old, light-coloured piece of clothing to dye (A clean cotton T-shirt works well. Ask an adult before dyeing anything.)*
o *dye ingredients (see the box on this page)*
o *a measuring cup*
o *a sieve*
o *alum (buy in hardware stores)*
o *cream of tartar (buy in grocery stores)*
o *a wooden spoon*

1. Put on some old clothes and cover the counter and floor with newspapers. Dye often splatters.

2. Put the piece of clothing you want to dye into a pot and cover it with water. Remove the thing you want to dye and set it aside.

3. Put your dye ingredients into the pot. See the box on this page for some ideas. The more you use, the darker your dye will be.

4. Put the pot on the stove. Bring the liquid to a boil. Turn the heat down and let it simmer for at least 20 minutes.

5. When you're satisfied with the colour of your dye, let it cool so that it's warm but not hot. Get an adult to help you strain off loose bits by pouring the dye through a sieve. (If the dye isn't dark enough, cheat. Add food colouring drop by drop until you like the colour.)

6. For 4 L (16 cups) of dye, you'll need about 15 mL (1 tablespoon) of alum and 60 mL (4 tablespoons) of cream of tartar. Measure them into the pot and stir well. (If you used more or less water, adjust the amount of alum and cream of tartar.)

7. Put the clothing you're going to dye into the pot and stir it with the wooden spoon so the colour won't streak. Leave it until it's a little darker than you want. The colour will be lighter when it's dry.

8. Rinse the material in cool water in a sink (if it's stainless steel) or in a bucket of cool water. Keep rinsing until no more colour comes out. When it's time to wash your dyed piece of clothing, wash it separately in cool, soapy water so it won't fade too much.

DYE INGREDIENTS

Ancient Mediterranean dyers crushed the juice from thousands of sea snails to make a small amount of fine purple dye. Other dyers scraped off the dried bodies of insects that lived on the bark of the kermes oak tree and made the insect bodies into a beautiful scarlet red colour called kermes.

You can try something simpler using these easy-to-find ingredients. Boil any of the following in 4 L (16 cups) of water:

- half a bread bag full of chestnut skins
- or the skins of 1.5 to 2 kg (3 to 4 pounds) onions
- or 250 mL (1 cup) purple rice
- or 1 kg (2 pounds) of beets
- or 8 teabags.

Put your best foot forward

Lotus-bud feet

Shoes like this look as if they should fit a two-year-old child. In fact, they used to be worn by wealthy women. For about a thousand years in China, people thought that tiny feet made a woman beautiful. When a girl was about five years old, each foot was bound tightly with cloth. The feet were kept wrapped for the rest of her life. The wrappings pulled her toes and heel together and forced her foot into a new shape. Girls and women with these lotus-bud feet often couldn't walk or even stand for long by themselves. They needed help from servants who, of course, didn't have bound feet.

CHOPINES

SHOES FOR LOTUS-BUD FEET

People throughout the ages have gone to real lengths—and heights and breadths—to show that they're wearing the latest style. Have a look at some of the different shoes people have put on their feet.

Get the point?

About 600 years ago, these *poulaines* from Poland were the latest style all across Europe. The longer the pointy toes, the better—even though one English king threatened to make people pay a 40-pence fine if the tips were longer than 5 cm (2 inches). People didn't obey. Some wore tips about twice as long as their feet! Tripping must have been a problem until someone thought of fastening the tips to the knees with chains. People sometimes also sewed little bells to the tips. That's where "rings on her fingers and bells on her toes" comes from.

Stilt shoes

About 500 years ago, wealthy European girls and women started wearing *chopines* to keep their shoes out of the mud in bad weather. But what started off as low, wooden clogs ended up as decorated platforms that were more like stilts than shoes. Women who wore high *chopines* needed help walking too.

MAKE YOUR OWN STILT SHOES

You'll need:

o *2 big empty juice cans (1.36 L/ 48 ounces) with one end still on*
o *a sturdy screwdriver*
o *a hammer*
o *2 pieces of light rope, each about 2 m (2 yards) long (exactly how long will depend on how tall you are)*
o *acrylic paints, brush, water (optional)*

1. Make two holes opposite one another near the closed end of each can. To make a hole, lay the can on the floor and get a friend to hold one end. Put the tip of the screwdriver at the other end, where you want the hole to be. Give the screwdriver a gentle whack or two with the hammer.

2. Make the holes big enough for the rope to go through. Use the screwdriver to bend the rough edges in so the rope won't

catch on them. Run a rope through the holes in each can.

3. Set your cans side by side. Pick up the ends of one rope. Step up on your cans. Figure out where to tie the ends of the rope together. The rope loop should be tight when you pull up with your arm slightly bent. Do the other rope.

4. If you want, remove the can labels and decorate your tin cans with acrylic paint. It sticks to metal.

5. Your stilts are ready. Pull the cans tight against your feet with the ropes and walk . . . slowly.

OUCH!

Why did people wear shoes that made walking difficult? Some peoples thought that if you didn't need to move, you didn't need to work for a living, so you must be well off and powerful. Others felt that walking slowly and gingerly made girls and women look beautiful. In China, this was called the willow walk.

Are things different today? Look at the high spike heels that some women wear to parties or even to their jobs. Why do women wear them? Why do men's dress-up shoes not hurt their feet and make walking difficult? What do you think?

Roll your own beads...

Gold, silver, copper, bronze. Glinting polished precious stones. Glass, clay, china. Stamped leather, silken threads. Feathers, flowers, seeds, seashells. Ostrich eggshells, deer toenails. Carved horn, shark teeth, puffin beaks. Bone, claws and hard black beetle shells. These are just a few of the things people have strung around their necks or sewn into fringes on their clothes. Why?

Rich or poor or somewhere in between, people everywhere have always longed to decorate their bodies, to show their status and whatever wealth they've had. Even when people have worn little or no clothing, they have always worn beads or some other kind of decoration.

Roll some beads yourself out of richly coloured paper. They won't add to your wealth but they may well add to your beauty.

You'll need:

○ *paper with deep colours and a shiny surface such as catalogue or magazine pages, wrapping paper, foil with paper backing*
○ *a thin rod like a shish-ke-bob skewer or the narrow end of a chopstick*
○ *scissors*
○ *white glue*
○ *heavy thread*
○ *a needle*

1. For this kind of necklace, you'll need wide and narrow beads. Cut wide triangles and narrow rectangles about the sizes shown on page 71.

2. Roll each triangle into a tube. To do this, roll the triangle around the shish-ke-bob skewer or chopstick. Start rolling at the wide end of the triangle as shown below.

...and string them

3. Glue the tip of the triangle down and slide the bead off the skewer or chopstick.

4. When all your beads are made, paint them with a white glue and water mixture. (Just make a mixture that's half glue and half water.) The glue coating will be tough and clear when it dries. Clean your brush before the glue dries.

5. Choose one of the necklace patterns. Lay out your wide and narrow beads, copying the pattern that you chose.

6. Cut a length of thread that stretches from fingertip to fingertip when you open your arms wide. If you run out while you're stringing the beads, tie another piece on and hide the knot inside a bead.

7. Tie a knot around the first bead to keep it from slipping off and start stringing.

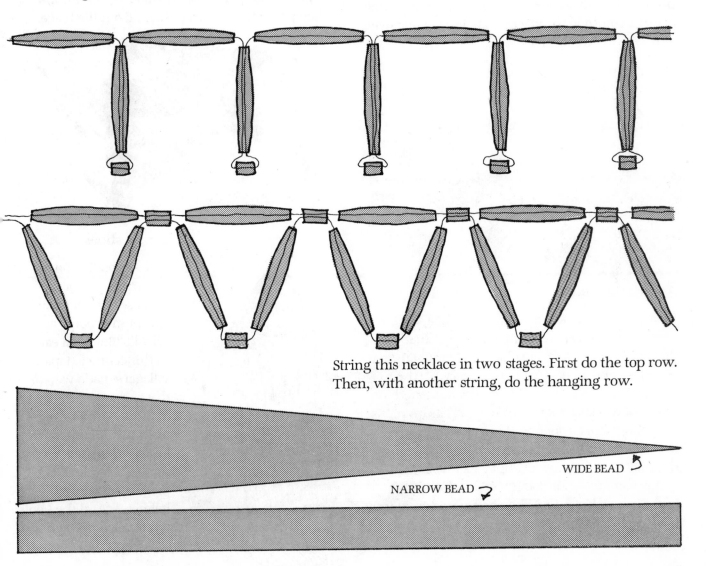

String this necklace in two stages. First do the top row. Then, with another string, do the hanging row.

WIDE BEAD

NARROW BEAD

Clothes that protect

Try listing all the ways you protect your body from the weather. For a start, how about sunglasses, raincoats, waterproof boots, down jackets and mitts? Now add all the ways people protect themselves in dangerous jobs or rough sports — such as wearing spacesuits, pressurized diving suits or hockey pads.

We often use new materials like plastic to make protective clothing. But long before these materials became common, people invented ingenious ways of protecting themselves.

A portable home

Wearing a *kepenek* is a little like being a snail. You carry your own small home with you. That's exactly what Turkish shepherds need when they have to spend all day out in the rain with their sheep. A *kepenek* is made from thick, matted wool felt. It's stiff enough to stand on its own. It's big enough that a shepherd can crouch inside. Even in heavy rain, he stays dry. The only drawback? A *kepenek* doesn't repel water. It soaks water in—but doesn't let it leak through. Sometimes a *kepenek* gets so heavy with rain that the shepherd gets a donkey to carry it for him.

The layered look

Three hundred years ago, in the Japanese city of Edo, fires broke out so often that they were called "flowers of Edo." Firefighters kept the fires from spreading by pulling down the nearby wooden houses with long hooks. Their uniforms were thick, made of many layers of cloth. These layered uniforms dulled the blows from falling debris. And, soaked with water by a pumpman, they protected the firefighters from the blaze.

Straw shoes

Unless you live on a farm, you probably don't see much straw except in brooms and whisks. But until early in this century, Japanese villagers made warm, dry snow boots and hats out of thick layers of straw and other grasses. The hats were sometimes called *yuki kabuto* or "snow helmets." And the boots were called *fuka gutsu* or "deep shoes."

Rabbit holes

This parka and these leggings are full of holes. You could stick your fingers right through them, yet the clothes are very warm. They used to be made by the northernmost Indians of North America who needed protection against long harsh winters. They would take rabbit skins and cut them in spirals, from the outside edge to the middle, to make long narrow strips. They twisted each strip so that it was furry all round. And then they wove the strips loosely to make clothing that was furry inside and out. Why was it so warm? Because the gaps in the warm fur trapped the heat of the body.

Black eyes

These ancient Egyptian men and women outlined their eyes with a black paint that they called *mesdemet*. They made it by grinding a kind of lead into a powder and mixing it with fat or resin. It made their eyes look striking and stylish. It may also have protected their eyes from the glaring desert sun, like the line of dark grease which modern football players draw below their eyes. Why does it work? The dark colour absorbs the bright sunlight instead of reflecting it into the eyes.

Wearing a kayak

Paddling a kayak can mean getting wet, and in icy Arctic waters, getting wet means getting cold. Long ago, the Inuit solved the problem by making shells from the linings of seal intestines. Gutskins are waterproof but they're narrow. Many had to be sewn together with special waterproof seams to make a whole shell. The hood and sleeves fastened tightly around the face and wrists. And the wide bottom was tied around the opening of the kayak. The paddler stayed dry in rain and high waves—and even if the kayak turned over.

73

Armed to the teeth

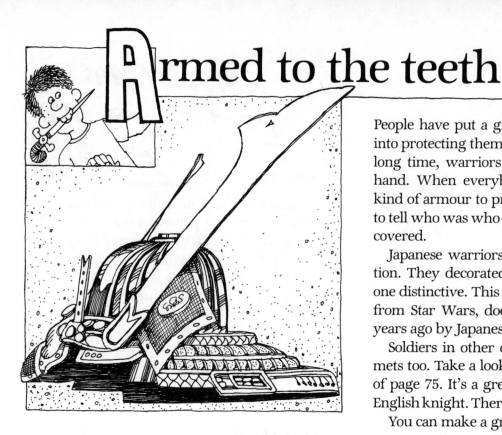

People have put a great deal of thought and skill into protecting themselves from one another. For a long time, warriors fought most battles hand to hand. When everybody was wearing the same kind of armour to protect themselves, it was hard to tell who was who—especially if their faces were covered.

Japanese warriors came up with a clever solution. They decorated their helmets to make each one distinctive. This one looks a bit like something from Star Wars, doesn't it? Yet it was worn 400 years ago by Japanese samurai.

Soldiers in other countries decorated their helmets too. Take a look at the helmet on the bottom of page 75. It's a great helm worn by a medieval English knight. There'd be no mistaking its wearer. You can make a great helm of your own.

You'll need:

o *a whole sheet of Bristol board*
o *aluminum foil*
o *clear tape*
o *brass fasteners*
o *sharp scissors*
o *brightly coloured tissue paper*
o *a friend*

1. Cover a sheet of Bristol board with foil, shiny side out. Tape it in place.

2. Roll the Bristol board, foil side out, into a tube that fits comfortably around your head. Get a friend to hold the tube so it doesn't spring open. Take it off and fasten it together with about 5 brass fasteners.

3. Put the tube on again with the join at the back of your head. Get your friend to mark where to cut so the tube will sit comfortably on your shoulders.

4. Take the tube off and cut out the shoulder pieces.

74

5. Put the tube back on and have your friend mark mouth and eye slits.

6. Remove the brass fasteners and cut out the slits. Decorate your helmet (see the box on this page). When you're done, roll the helm back into a tube again and put in the brass fasteners.

7. Make cuts about 15 cm (6 inches) long straight down from the top of your helm. Make them about 15 cm (6 inches) apart. Cut each flap into a triangle.

8. Fold these flaps down, one on top of the other, and tape them down.

9. Cut out strips of tissue paper for plumes and twist the ends together.

10. Tape the twist on top of your helm with the ends hanging over the front. Flip the loose ends back so that they arch back over the helm.

SHOW WHO YOU ARE

One English prince, the Black Prince, wore a crest of a ferocious-looking lion on top of his great helm. Symbols like this showed who was wearing the helm. So did brightly coloured plumes or patterns painted right on the helm. Decorate your helm to show who you are. Invent symbols or designs that stand for you or your family. You might want to try a symbol that represents your name. Long ago a knight named Keeble might use a key and a bell, while someone called Breakspear might use a broken spear.

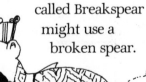

Transform yourself...

Do you remember the first time you saw someone wearing a mask? What about the first time you put on a mask yourself? Did you act the way you always do? Chances are you didn't.

Stand in front of a mirror and look at your face. Now make as many different faces as you can — happy, sad, thoughtful, tricky, angry, jealous, peaceful — and watch how your features move. Your face changes as often as your feelings change.

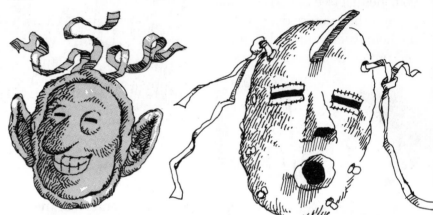

You'll need:

- aluminum foil (the heavy, wide kind is best)
- scissors
- scotch tape or masking tape
- acrylic paints
- a paper plate
- a paint brush
- a container filled with water
- 2 pieces of string, each about 30 cm (12 inches) long
- white glue
- decorations such as yarn, buttons, bottle caps, coloured foil, tissue paper, feathers, glitter

1. Cut a piece of foil about 70 cm (28 inches) long. Fold it in half, end to end.

2. Make a face that goes with the feeling or animal you've chosen. You might scrunch up your nose, bare your teeth, suck in your cheeks or relax your face.

3. Centre the foil over your face. Then, starting around your eyes and nose, gently press it into the

nooks and crannies. Before you run out of breath, lift the foil off your face.

4. Look at your mask and see where it needs shape. Put the foil back on your face and press some more. Keep shaping the mask until you're satisfied.

5. Fold over the outer edges of the mask to make them smooth and strong.

6. Exaggerate the mask's features by pressing against the inside of the mask. For example, if you want bulging eyes, gently push the eyes out more. Now you can decorate your mask. Tape pieces of doubled-over foil to the edges of your mask to make a mane, crest, huge ears or other unusual features.

... put on a mask

Masks are different. They show only one feeling or expression. Often the features are exaggerated to make that expression easy to see.

People all over the world have worn masks to transform themselves for many reasons — to hon-our or ask for help from gods, to frighten evil spirits away, to cure illness, to help tell a story or act out a play or to disguise themselves for fun. Transform yourself. Make a mask that shows one feeling or perhaps an animal that you really like.

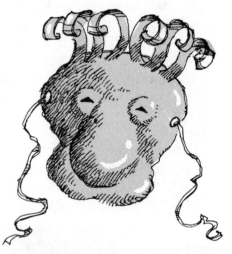

7. Cut tiny slits in the mask where your eyes, nose and mouth are. Gently rip and fold the edges of the slits back inside the mask until the holes are the right size. Tape the edges down so they won't cut you.

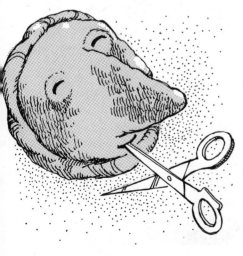

8. Poke little holes for strings on either side of the mask, about the same level as the eyes. Tape around all the edges and holes on the inside of the mask to make it stronger.

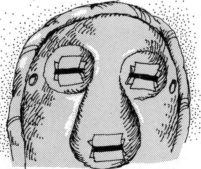

9. Paint your mask. You might leave some foil showing for effect. Let the paint dry.
10. Glue on any other objects or materials you like.

11. Thread the short strings through the small holes on either side of the mask. Knot them to make ties.

Put on your mask and imagine yourself inside the animal or feeling you made. For example, if you made a fox mask, you might say: I am a fox. I am sleek and swift and cunning. I am not afraid at night. Say whatever enters your head. You may be surprised at what you discover about your mask — and about yourself.

Beware the evil eye!

Have you ever carried a four-leaf clover or rabbit's foot in your pocket? If you have, you were doing something people have been doing for a very long time: trying to make sure your luck was good. To many people today and in the past, inviting good luck isn't enough. You also need to protect yourself from evil spirits that bring sickness, bad weather and bad luck. Here are some symbols that people have used to guard against evil or to bring good luck.

Bat luck

Do bats bring good luck or bad? In China, the word for bat is "fu." It sounds the same as the word for good luck or blessings. Wearing a collar embroidered with bats is meant to bring you good luck.

If looks could kill . . .

Why is this camel wearing blue beads on its harness? Not for decoration. Its North African owner is protecting it against the evil eye. He's not the only one who fears the evil eye. In almost every part of the world, people have believed that a mean, envious look can hurt or even kill.

A bowlful of demons

Bowls like this weren't meant for food. Two thousand years ago in what's now Iraq, people buried them, upside-down, under the floors of their houses. Why? A magical spell was written inside each bowl to frighten demons and devils away. And, archaeologists think, the bowl was meant to trap any demons that weren't scared off by the spell.

Armed with amulets

The ancient Egyptians wore small charms or amulets to drive away evil or give themselves strength. Udjat-eye amulets that looked like this were popular. The udjat eye was the eye of Horus, the falcon god. According to an Egyptian myth, Horus fought with his uncle, Seth, and lost an eye. Another god gave Horus back his eye and his sight. Because of this, the udjat became a sign of being whole and unharmed by evil spirits.

You can make your own amulet and see if it works for you.

You'll need:

o *baker's clay (see page 90)*
o *a pencil with a sharp point or a meat skewer*
o *a baking sheet*
o *an egg flipper*
o *acrylic paints*
o *a brush*
o *a jar*
o *ribbon or string*

1. Decide what you're going to make. You might make:
o something to protect you, like an udjat eye or a favourite animal. You might want to try a cat: Bastet the cat goddess watched over many ancient Egyptian houses
o something that shows what you'd like more of, like a tiny strong arm for strength, a heart for love or courage or a foot for speed.

2. Mix the baker's clay using the recipe on page 90.

3. Shape a piece of clay into an amulet no more than 0.5 cm (1/8 inch) thick. To join two pieces of clay, put a drop of water at the joint and press them together.

4. Use the sharp point of a pencil or skewer to poke a hole in the amulet so that you can hang it on a string later.

5. Lift the amulet gently onto a baking sheet with an egg flipper.

6. Heat the oven to 300° F. Bake the amulet for 20 to 30 minutes. Ask an adult to help you take the baking sheet out of the oven. Let the amulet cool.

7. Paint your amulet and let the paints dry. Put the cord through the hole and tie the ends together. Wear your amulet around your neck or carry it in your pocket. Enjoy your good luck!

Leave your mark...

Whenever you write your name on something you own, you're making sure that others know it's yours. People have left their mark as long as they have had things to claim as their own. The ancient Egyptians, for example, tied a roll of parchment or papyrus with a string, pressed a small lump of clay over the knot and stamped it with a seal. They sealed jars, bundles of goods, even doors to storage rooms in the same way.

You can make a wearable seal of your own — a seal ring.

You'll need:

- o *brass fastener like this*
- o *a small cup-shaped mould such as the little cups that hold box chocolates or an egg carton cup*
- o *plaster of Paris (see page 91)*
- o *carving tools such as a big nail, plastic knife, fine sandpaper*
- o *sealing wax or coloured wax candle*

1. Open the forks of the brass fastener and bend it into a loose ring around your finger. Adjust the fit later.

2. Mix the plaster and pour it quickly into the mould.

3. Stick the flat top of your brass-fastener ring into the plaster until it's covered. Then push it in a little further.
4. Let the plaster dry. It takes about half an hour. Then peel the mould off the ring.

5. For about 24 hours after the plaster dries, it will be easy to carve. Use your tools to cut or scratch deep patterns in the plaster. Use sandpaper to smoothe the rough spots.
6. Put a blob of melted wax on the sealed edge of an envelope and press your seal into it.

...put your stamp on it

BREAK INTO THAT LETTER!

Whoever heard of an envelope that you have to smash—not rip—to get the contents out? The people who lived in the Near East, in Mesopotamia, certainly did. About 5000 years ago, they invented a kind of writing called cuneiform. To write, they used a special stick to make wedge-shaped marks on damp clay tablets. When they wanted to send a tablet to someone else, they put it in an envelope of clay, closed it up and marked it with a seal.

Their seals weren't stamps or rings. They were small stone cylinders about the size of a little battery and carved all over with tiny pictures and cuneiform writing.

The pictures and writing on the seals tell archaeologists a lot about how Mesopotamians lived.

What did it take to become a seal-maker who could carve such tiny fine designs? Training, patience—and short-sightedness. Why? In those days, there were no magnifying glasses. But if you were short-sighted, your eyes worked as built-in magnifying glasses.

New fun with old games

Here are two games that will take you back in time (or at least help you pass the time).

Chien-tze ("*jee-en-dzuh*")

Kick a small weight up into the air over and over again and you're playing an old game that's been played in many parts of the world. Chinese children in Taiwan used to kick *chien-tze* birdies made from paper and a coin with a hole in the middle. Polish children kicked *Zoshka* or *Sophie*, a little lead weight with a pompom of wool. So did Korean children; they called it jay-gee. In North America, Native children filled small buckskin balls with sand, pebbles, or seeds. Maybe you play Hacky Sack with a beanbag. Here's how to make a *chien-tze* style birdie yourself.

You'll need:

○ *a metal washer about 2.5 cm (1 inch) across*
○ *tissue paper*
○ *a sharp pencil*

1. Cut a rectangle of tissue paper about 15 cm by 22 cm (6 inches by 8½ inches).

2. Put the washer in the middle of one long edge of the paper. Fold the paper and the washer over and over smoothly and tightly.

3. Use the pencil point very gently to poke a hole through the paper in the middle of the washer.

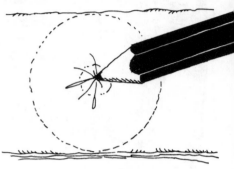

4. Feed the ends of the paper through the centre of the washer.

5. Trim the ends of the strips so they're both about 7 cm (3 inches) long and open them up a bit. Rip them into narrow strips as shown.

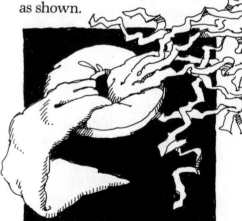

6. Drop your birdie onto your foot as shown. See how many times you can kick it up without dropping it. This may seem impossible at first but don't give up.

Nine Men's Morris
(for 2 players)

Test your wits. Play Nine Men's Morris, the same game that hooked Roman soldiers, Viking kings and British settlers who came to North America.

We still know how to play Nine Men's Morris because the rules were never lost. We also know that people have been playing it for at least 3400 years. The oldest known Morris board was carved into the roof of an ancient Egyptian temple, probably by the workers who were building it.

You'll need:

○ a board (draw a big version of the board on the right)
○ 2 sets of 9 "men." Each set of 9 should be a different colour (Dimes and pennies work well; so do two kinds of beans.)

1. You play Morris on the 24 "points" of the board. See the picture on this page for how to draw the board and find the points.
2. Take turns putting your men on the board one at a time. You can put a man on any empty point.
3. Once all the men are on the board, take turns moving them. In one turn, you can move one

of your men one space along a line to an empty point. The object is to make a "mill." A mill is formed when you have three men side by side in a row like this: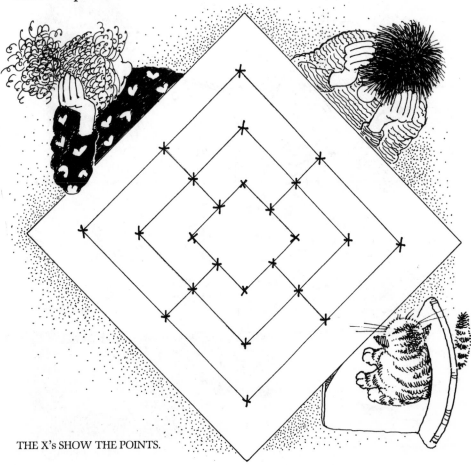
4. When you have made a mill, you can remove one of your friend's men. This is called "pounding." Your goal is to pound (remove) as many of your friend's men as possible. You can pound any of your opponent's men except one that's in a mill.

5. Once you've made a mill, you don't have to keep it whole. If you move a man out of a mill, you can move it back again in any later turn. Then you get to pound another of your friend's men.

6. If the only men that your friend has left are in a mill, you can pound them.

7. You win when none of your friend's men can move or when you've pounded all but two of them.

THE X's SHOW THE POINTS.

Solve a crushing problem

Chew on a cocoa bean. It's not nearly as tasty as sipping a cup of cocoa, is it? Many foods can't be eaten unless they're ground up first. Hunt through your kitchen. See how many foods you can find that need to be ground up, are already ground up or are made with ground-up ingredients.

How did all those ground-up foods get ground up? Mostly by large grinding machines in mills or bakeries. But for thousands of years, it was a different story. Grinding food was part of everyday life —and it was done by hand.

Grind up some hais

Hais is an ancient version of trail mix from North Africa. Nomads ate it as they travelled. They needed food that wouldn't spoil, was nourishing, easy to carry and filling.

Hais was made by grinding bread, dates and nuts into little pieces and forming them into balls. Make hais yourself but do the grinding the old way, by hand. It's up to you to figure out how. Food processors and blenders and other electrical grinders are out of bounds! As you'll find out, *hais* is delicious, but a little goes a long way.

You'll need:
- *50 mL (¼ cup) pistachio nuts*
- *50 mL (¼ cup) dates*
- *50 mL (¼ cup) shelled almonds*
- *50 mL (¼ cup) dry breadcrumbs*
- *a spoonful of cooking oil (The old recipe calls for sesame oil — buy it at health food stores.)*
- *powdered sugar (optional)*

1. Remove the pistachio nuts from their shells.
2. If the dates are hard, soak them in a little warm water to soften them. Remove the pits.
3. Crush, pound or grind up the dates, almonds and pistachios until the pieces are about the size of rice grains. Mix them all together.
4. Mix in the breadcrumbs and add just enough oil to make things stick together.
5. Form the mixture into little balls. Sprinkle them with powdered sugar if you wish. Eat.

WHAT A GRIND!

Archaeologists have found grinding tools all over the world. Why? Every family or village needed to grind food, especially grain. So grinding tools were common.

Often they were made from materials that last, like stone. Not just any stone would do for grinding. Smooth stones slipped. Gritty stones grabbed and cut much better. The only problem was that tiny bits of grit broke off and got into the food. Skulls from the past show the result: worn down teeth.

Here are a few ways people solved the grinding problem in the past.

This Huron Indian woman used a pestle and mortar to pound dried corn kernels into flour. The mortar was made by hollowing out a tree trunk. The pestle was a smooth wooden pole.

This ancient Egyptian rocked back and forth when he used this stone saddle quern. The ground flour trickled down the slanted stone and gathered at the bottom.

Once people figured out that grinding stones could move round and round (and not just back and forth), they got donkeys to do the work for them.

Time for supper...

Picture yourself and your family transported back 700 years through time to the great hall of a medieval European lord just as supper is being served. This is what you might see. You'll notice that these people are eating without forks or plates. Turn the page to find out how to try it yourself.

Medieval dog food didn't come out of a can. These dogs are gnawing on bones and table scraps.

Why is this man scratching his head? People's hair and clothes were often infested with bugs. Not exactly pleasant dinner companions.

Only the lord, lady and important guests are sitting "above the salt" — that is, at the raised high table with the fancy salt cellar, or "nef." Everyone else is sitting "below the salt." In those days, salt was rare and precious. The less important you were, the farther you had to sit from the salt and the poorer the food you were served.

You'll notice there were no plates. Instead people used thick slices of stale bread called "trenchers." Diners heaped food onto the trenchers from a big serving dish and ate them (or tossed them to the dogs) when they got soggy.

...700 years ago

This woman has brought her own pointed knife to the table for spearing food and cutting it into little pieces. She'll use a spoon too for runny soups and sauces. But she wouldn't think of using a fork, even though cooks used big forks in the kitchen. Europeans didn't use table forks until about 400 years ago. Even 100 years ago, the British navy didn't let their sailors use knives and forks: they were considered sissy.

Freshly cut, sweet-smelling rushes were strewn on the floor before the meal and swept up after. Why? They soaked up spills and scraps tossed from the table.

There's food for two in this bowl, or "cover." Only the lord or a very important guest would get a dish all to himself.

There were lots of servants around to get dinner on the table. The pantler got his name from the Latin word for bread: "panis." He made all the bread plates or trenchers and kept diners supplied with new ones as the old ones became soggy. You probably wouldn't want the sewer's and the cup-bearer's jobs. Besides serving the food and keeping everyone's cup full, they had to taste all the lord's food and drink. Why? To make sure that it wasn't poisoned.

Bread plates...

Eating without a fork is a challenge if you're not used to it. But many peoples, past and present, have used only their fingers to pick up their food. Eating with your fingers isn't the only thing that's different about a medieval-style meal as you'll discover when you serve one. By the time you put food on the table, you'll have done the jobs of more than five people: the pantler, the cook, the ewerer (water-pourer), the sewer (server), the cupbearer and kitchen servants.

You'll need:

○ *newspapers*
○ *unsliced bread, a few days old*
○ *a bread knife*
○ *2 cups of water*
○ *2 spoons*
○ *some stew*
○ *a bowl big enough to hold food for two*
○ *a pitcher of water*
○ *a large bowl or dishpan*

1. Spread newspapers on the floor around the table. They'll take the place of freshly cut rushes.

2. Make bread trenchers by cutting slices of bread 2.5 cm (1 inch) thick.

3. Set the table for two, with a cup of water, a spoon and a bread trencher at each place.

4. Fill a bowl with stew and set it between the two trenchers. This is your "cover."

5. Take turns pouring water over your hands and into the spare bowl. When you eat with your fingers, you want to start clean.

6. Dip into the cover with your fingers and put some food onto your trencher. Eat the food on your trencher with your fingers. Use the spoon to get at the sauce.

7. Eat your trencher when you're done or throw it to the dog, if you have one.

...and finger foods

WHAT'S FOR SUPPER?

In the Middle Ages in Europe, what you ate depended on who you were. If you were poor, you'd probably have a chunk of dark bread, some cheese and some soupy vegetable stew from a pot that was always cooking over the fire. You'd never have much meat.

If you were rich, you'd eat more meat than anything else. Your cooks would serve bite-sized chunks of meat with spice-flavoured sauces. You wouldn't think much of fruit and vegetables. Unless they were in a meat dish, they were considered food for the poor.

MIND YOUR MANNERS, MEDIEVAL-STYLE

Try sharing a cover with a friend. Then see if the advice of these medieval writers makes sense.

Do not spit across the table.

"Thou must not put either thy fingers into thine ears, or thy hands to thy head. The man who is eating must not be cleaning by scraping with his fingers at any foul part."

"If it happen that you cannot help scratching, then courteously take a portion of your dress, and scratch with that. That is more befitting than that your skin should become soiled."

Do not "poke about everywhere when thou hast meat or eggs or some such dish. He who turns or pokes about on the platter, searching, is unpleasant, and annoys his neighbour at dinner."

Once you've gnawed on a bone, don't put it back in the dish. Drop it on the floor.

Don't lick the dish.

Useful recipes

ROM PLAY DOUGH

You'll need:

○ *a large bowl*
○ *a measuring cup*
○ *250 mL (1 cup) flour*
○ *50 mL (¼ cup) salt*
○ *30 mL (2 tablespoons) cream of tartar (the magic ingredient)*
○ *15 mL (1 tablespoon) cooking oil*
○ *5 mL (1 teaspoon) food colouring*
○ *250 mL (1 cup) boiling water*

1. Mix the flour, salt and cream of tartar in a bowl.

2. Pour the oil, food colouring and water into the measuring cup.

3. Pour the liquid into the dry ingredients and stir. Soon the mixture will turn into a ball. Let it cool till it's not too hot to touch. Use your hands to knead the dough ball until it feels smooth.

4. Store the dough in an airtight plastic container. It will last for 3 to 5 months.

5. Leave the thing you make in the air to dry. It air-dries hard. For an extra shine, coat it with a half-and-half mixture of white glue and water. Or paint it. (If you're using water-based paints, don't coat the paint with glue and water; the paint will smear and run.)

BAKER'S CLAY

You'll need:

○ *a large bowl*
○ *500 mL (2 cups) all-purpose flour*
○ *250 mL (1 cup) table salt*
○ *175 mL (¾ cup) water*
○ *30 mL (2 tablespoons) glycerine*

1. Measure the flour and the salt into a large bowl and mix.

2. Add the water and glycerine and stir until mixed.

3. Knead the clay for 3 or 4 minutes until it's smooth.

4. If you wish, you can add food colouring to the clay when you're mixing it, or paint it when it's baked with acrylic paints. Bake it at 300°F until it's lightly brown and hard.

PLASTER OF PARIS

You'll need:

o *a mixing can, bucket or bowl*
o *125 mL (½ cup) cold water*
o *80 mL (⅓ cup) fast-setting plaster of Paris*
o *a spoon or stick for stirring*
o *a mould*

1. Put the water into your bucket. You can double or triple the quantity of water and plaster of Paris as needed.
2. Sprinkle the plaster powder into the water and stir. The mixture will thicken very quickly.
3. Pour it into your mould right away. If you haven't made enough, mix up another batch and pour it on top of the first.
4. Plaster heats up and then cools down as it dries. When it's completely cool and firm to the touch, rip or tear away the mould.
5. Wash your equipment in water before the plaster dries.

ACRYLIC PAINTS

These bright, water-based paints have one big advantage: they will stick to metal. The less expensive "junior" variety works well for projects. To make acrylic paint last longer, add a little acrylic gel. Or make a half-and-half mixture of ordinary tempera paints and acrylic gel. Clean brushes with water before they dry.

Where to find ingredients

acrylic paints: artists' supplies and craft stores.
alum (non-toxic): potassium alum, available in large drugstores, is best; pickling alum, in grocery stores, is okay.
beads: sewing, craft or specialty bead supply shops.
cream of tartar: grocery stores.
foil with paper backing: gift wrap or craft stores.
glycerine: drugstores.
grey duct tape: hardware stores.
plaster of Paris: hardware stores.

Glossary

Amulet: something worn as a charm against bad luck.

Archaeologist: a scientist who studies people from the past.

Botanist: a scientist who studies plants.

Entomologist: a scientist who studies insects.

Fossils: the preserved remains of plants and animals that died long ago.

Nocturnal: active at night.

Palaeobotanist: a scientist who studies fossil plants.

Palaeontologist: a scientist who studies fossils and ancient forms of life.

Trilobites: extinct marine creatures, now sometimes found as fossils.

CREDITS

Page 85: recipe for *hais* adapted from *Food in History* by Reay Tannahill. Used by permission of the publisher, Stein and Day.

Page 89: "Mind your manners" reprinted from *Food in History* by Reay Tannahill. Used by permission of the publisher, Stein and Day.

Activities and Experiments

Index

Answers

Go on a rot hunt, page 17

1. Light makes cloth fade. 2. Air pollution turns roofs green. 3. Mould causes the blue-black patches. 4. Light and air pollution make paper turn brittle or yellow.
5. Weathering by light and dust dulls paint, especially on cars. 6. Salt damage makes the white line. 7. Water and air pollution rust metal.

What's wrong with this picture, pages 20–21

These are the things that you wouldn't find in a living room in the year 1850: 1. a car, 2. Mickey Mouse, 3. an electric light, 4. a telephone, 5. pizza, 6. a toy robot, 7. the clock radio on the bookshelves, 8. a Walkman, 9. a model of an airplane, 10. sneakers.

Solve a bony puzzle, page 26–27

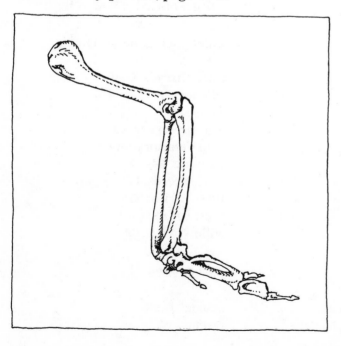

Flesh out a dinosaur skeleton, page 29

Here's what a Parasaurolophus probably looked like:

Hunt for the riches of the earth, pages 42–43

These things come from the earth: phone, pet cage, light, mirror, Walkman, aquarium, paints and piggy bank. They're all made of metal, glass, plastics or ground-up rock. The comics, sweatshirt, sneakers and wooden desk came not from the earth but from things that grew in the earth. In fact, so did everything else in this room. You could say that *everything* around us comes from the earth.

How much can a pot tell you?, page 51

This was the oldest pot:

This was the youngest pot: